A GREEK BLOODY DRAMA

Dino Kottis

Contents

To my wife, Melina.

A GREEK BLOODY DRAMA

Introduction

The Greek language is rich in proverbial phrases, which are commonly used in daily speech. Throughout the book you will come across a number of them. To aid you with your reading and understanding of these phrases, I have included their basic meaning. Being a Greek myself, I did my best with it so you can get a taste of the real Greek experience.

But there's one specific word that most foreigners learn when they explore our proud Greek nation. It is possibly the most frequently used word across all age groups and genders speaking the Greek language.

This is no other but the infamous word 'malaka'. This term seems to interlace itself with every other sentence us Greeks exchange with family, friends and any other humans in general. A swear word that managed to get into the mainstream and become part of our everyday life.

While many of us use it numerous times on a daily basis, only a modest amount of people is aware of the intriguing origins behind this captivating word that unifies all Greek souls worldwide. Imagine that even the younger members of the Greek diaspora, with their proficiency in the Greek language being usually limited, use the word 'malaka' with exceptional comfort at any given opportunity, in combination with English or French or any language they speak.

'Malaka' is a slang term which has a range of meanings. The literal translation of the word is the 'man who masturbates' and it is commonly used as an insult, similar to 'wanker' in UK English and 'jerk-off' in American English. However, the meaning of 'malaka' can change depending on the tone and context of its use. It can be used to express pleasure, horror, anger, affection and other emotions.

In addition to its literal meaning, 'malaka' can also mean any of the following: asshole / motherfucker / jerk / son of a bitch / douchebag or douche / sod / fucker / fuckhead / dickhead / cocksucker / shithead / git / tosser / ass or arse / bugger.

But it's not only drama and insults with 'malaka'. Conversely, depending on the context, it can just mean 'dude' or 'mate'. So, don't get hot-headed straight away when a Greek says to you: "Hey malaka, what's up?" They are honestly sweet with you and trying to be friendly.

But apart from all the above, it can also mean 'idiot', which is also commonly used in everyday speech. It is rare though for 'malaka' to be used in its literal meaning of 'man who masturbates'. I know, it's so confusing. So, you better check the tone of voice and body language, in combination with the situation you are in, to understand what kind of 'malaka' you are each time a Greek calls you one.

To dig a bit deeper in the word 'malaka', it has its origins from the word 'malakos' (μαλακός), which translates to 'soft' or 'spoilt, 'well-used to luxuries of life'. It's commonly used in its vocative case form, 'malaka' (μαλάκα) [ma'laka] and is a strictly masculine noun.

But the Greeks wanted to be fair to women. Therefore, they created the feminine form of the word, which is 'malako' (μαλάκω). To keep the women even happier, they also created the word 'malakismeni' (μαλακισμένη), which is a more vintage form of the word and is used as a slur.

This is Greek style Equality.

7:54pm, Thursday 13th May 2010

Tasos burst into the taverna. His heart was pounding like he had just escaped from the Minotaur's labyrinth in the city of Knossos in Crete. The voice inside his dizzy head was constantly speaking to him, trying to control his extremely sweaty body and guide it in the right direction. This sticky mess of a body had just done a terrible, very terrible thing for which the voice was giving him epic hell.

"Where's Babis?

You must find Babis now!

You need Babis!

Find him you idiot!

Go find him now malaka Tasos!"

To his utter surprise, the taverna was unexpectedly busy with all the tables full of people, which was rather odd for a Thursday night before 8pm. Under normal circumstances, the majority of the local customers from this Athenian suburb usually arrived there between 9:30pm to 10pm.

Consequently, Tasos expected that around this time on a Thursday night, the place should be nearly empty. He also knew that Babis would be setting up the tables in the customer seating area waiting for the hordes of hungry and thirsty locals to arrive.

He couldn't understand what he was missing. Was it a big Christian Orthodox celebration he forgot about? Or did Babis have an offer 2-for-1 meals for early birds? Nothing made sense to him, but he had no time to analyse this any further. He had messed everything up so royally that he needed to move faster than the speed of light. He was past the point of no return and '*ihe pari fotia o kolos tu*'. *(είχε πάρει φωτιά ο κώλος του) [literal translation: his ass was on fire. This colourful Greek phrase is used to describe extreme urgency.]*

The overcrowded taverna was a cloud of cigarette smoke, soon to be so thick that it would make it hard to see if someone was waving or making the wank gesture from across the room. The music was relatively loud and the customers' voices were even louder as their conversations were fighting to beat the unreasonably high volume .

This was utter chaos for him.

He immediately felt the sweat running down his spine and forehead, like someone turned on a cold-water tap attached to his body. His frightened eyes darted around the room, desperately searching for Babis. Three full seconds passed and still there was no sign of him. That was the exact moment when the redness of his face broke the World Red Face Record.

"What the absolute hell's going on in here?

Who are all these idiots?

Why are they here so early?

It's only Thursday for God's sake!" his inner voice had become totally irritated and completely squeaky.

And it wouldn't stop there.

"Every day.

And I mean every freaking day.

At the same time.

He's in this same bloody room.

Every freaking day.

With no exemption.

Where's this mahoosive teddy-bear robot today?

Now that you need him?

You malaka Tasos...

What did you do?

You stupid little piece of shit!

You waste of human skin!"

If someone could press their ear to his steaming hot skull, they might just be able to hear the echoes of the screams, trapped inside his boiling brain.

The last thing he wanted after his incredibly reckless actions a few minutes ago, was to be recognised by someone he knew and get trapped in a small talk. He thought that keeping his baseball cap and sunglasses on was a brilliant solution to have all the necessary cover he needed. Even if it was getting dark outside. He wasn't at the right state of mind to have a proper conversation with any human apart from Babis.

"Hey Tasos! Hey! Over here! Over here!" a man, sitting at a table in the other corner of the taverna, shouted at him with his hand raised.

"Oh God!

Shit.

Whyyyy??

Not this malaka now!" his inner voice screamed.

Instinctively, he pretended that he didn't hear anything or anyone calling him directly with his name. He immediately turned the other way around to get the hell out of the taverna as fast as possible. He came into the realisation that it would be wiser to use the back door after all, the one used by the staff and suppliers for deliveries.

But this made the man shout even louder. "Hey Tasos! Hey! Over here! Here! Hey!"

So much louder that it beat all the extreme noise in there and made everyone turn their heads towards the man's table. So much louder that it was impossible for Tasos to continue pretending that he didn't hear him.

"That's it.

Now I'm screwed.

Out of all the people…

 This specific malaka.

And it had to be now.

Why now..." he thought.

Tasos was a muscle-bound machine. He pounded the iron five times a week, with the sweat from his swollen muscles dripping onto the polished hardwood floor of the gym every single time. He was so obsessed with his body that he would do anything to achieve perfection.

He was driven by a strong sense of motivation after a rejection he received from a ripped woman he met at the same gym almost two years ago. *"You're not fit enough for me love. Work out hard and come back when you can count your abs."* was her response after he asked her for a date.

These two life-changing sentences were fixed in his brain ever since. Even if he had been working out for years, after that historical moment, his obsession had reached a new level. He was now spending hours every day in the gym, usually neglecting most of his other responsibilities. His friends and family were worried about him, but he refused to listen to any of them. He was determined to count his abs, regardless of the cost.

Spending hours at that gym, came with its side effects though. One of the most serious ones was meeting extremely annoying, brainless, massive blocks like this guy. He loathed this man and always tried to avoid any interaction with him whenever they met at the gym. Apart from the fact that the topics of his conversations were shockingly stupid, this man had a very loud voice. So loud that could leave you with a permanent hearing condition if you spoke with him for over five minutes in one go. And he was a cop and a neo-Nazi too.

So, Tasos had no other choice but to turn around, towards the cop's direction. The same exact moment his inner voice said: *"Tora ton ipiame..." (Τώρα τον ήπιαμε) [literal translation: Now we drank him. This phrase is used by Greeks to describe a scenario when something gets completely out of hand and everything takes the wrong turn.]*

"How's things my man? Did you go to the gym today? I didn't have time. I was busy with my girl earlier today. If you know what I mean!" said the massive cop and right after he finished his sentence, he turned his head, which was so huge that it could have its own gravitational pull, and winked his right eye to the lizard-looking bimbo sitting next to him.

Almost all the customers in the room were watching the entire scene as the cop's voice continued being incredibly loud. And they must have all been thinking the exact same thing: "*What a mega-malaka is this!*"

"Come on my friend! Sit down and have a glass of wine with us!" proposed the cop and pushed a chair from his table to make room for Tasos to sit. But his eyes focused on Tasos' trousers. "What's all this mess on your pants? What happened to you mate? Is it bird shit?"

When Tasos listened to the neo-Nazi cop's comment, he headed towards a panic attack. The sweat was now rushing out of every pore of his skin. His face took the same expression most babies take when they're having a poop: their face goes totally red and looks like they're smiling. But in reality, they're pushing the poop with all their power to force it out of their bum, which results in a fake smile.

And that's how he responded to the cop. No words, no gestures, just a 'pooping baby smile'. This was the best he could do.

He then turned his 'disguised', flaming red head towards the passage which connected the customer seating area with the bar area at the back.

"*This is where you need go!*

This is where Babis must be!" ordered the inner voice and then yelled again: "*Screw the neo-Nazi malaka and run!*"

The distance between Tasos' current location in the taverna and the bar area where Babis would probably be, was about thirty feet. With the urgency included, it shouldn't take him longer than four seconds to cover. So, he accelerated at full speed and left the brainless, massive, neo-Nazi cop with the mouth open, watching him drifting away.

He zigzagged around the tables like a cheetah, trying to avoid crushing on the customers who were already sitting there. He had to cross four full tables to reach to the next room. He did very well until the fourth table, which was right next to the bar area entrance. When he finally made it there and felt like a champ...

BANG!

He crushed with an object of monumental size which was moving close to the speed of sound. This was fast and furious Babis who was carrying a tray full of empty water glasses on his left hand and a glass jug full of water on the right.

The three seconds following the crush can be summarised as follows: for one second, they stared into each other eyes intensely. Tasos looked at Babis with stupendous accomplishment for finding him, but also with overwhelming fear. Babis looked at Tasos with mega-shock and tons of anger for what would follow this moronic crash.

After the first impact, Babis, being a very experienced waiter for years, managed to keep back control of the tray with the glasses, after it had literally flown in the air. Apart from one rebel glass, which followed its own destiny. This one initially landed on Tasos' burning head and then down on the tiled floor, where it smashed into one thousand pieces...

"Opa!" cheered one of the customers. "Yiamas!" another one joyfully cried right afterwards. A third one followed by shouting "Bravo! What a show!" and then everyone in the taverna burst out laughing.

A kilo of lamb chops, one beef burger stuffed with feta and one pork sausage

Babis was the main owner and General Manager of the taverna. His destiny was to serve people and it seemed like he was enjoying it a lot. At least that's how it looked like from the outside as his interactions with the customers were always uplifting and pleasant.

But deep inside, he had reached the point of being totally fed up running around like an oversized clown, trying to make everyone happy. He believed that he was made for bigger things than serving food and drinks, but he struggled to practically support this belief.

Completing high school was a formidable challenge for him as he wasn't the brightest bulb in the chandelier. As a student, he was usually invisible in the class and never completed any of his homework. Going to school every day proved to be pointless as he was returning home with the same knowledge he had, when he left in the morning. In other words, during most of his school time, he learned just enough to be able to read, write and complete basic mathematic calculations. School education wasn't this boy's forte.

That's why his parents, Ilias and Soula, didn't push him towards any academic direction, like university studies or any kind of study outside the basic education he received in school. Part of the blame was theirs as well, as they never put any decent effort to develop this slow-burning engine to reach its full potential.

Therefore, when he was sixteen years old, he started working in cafés, restaurants, bars and clubs in the local area. And he was smashing it from the early days, as he was very outgoing, highly social and funny. Many of the customers seemed to like interacting with him a lot. When he was working, his energy was phenomenal and could easily cover the work of two or even three waiters. And that's how he built his professional image and value as one of the top waiters in the local area.

His upbeat mood made him a customers' favourite, especially amongst the female population. This was due to his sweet and harmless approach with all women. He never tried to get them drunk or load them with bullshit so he could take advantage of them. Unlike most of his male friends, who were mainly targeting to get a quick and easy one-night-stand at every given opportunity.

 He was very polite and protective with women of any age and that's the reason he could be seen having coffees or drinks with the most beautiful females of the town. Therefore, several local men, most of them being professional wankers, had become envious and used to call him a *'kalinihtakia'. (καληνυχτάκια) [literal translation: a goodnight-guy. This is used in Greece for those men who escort a woman to her house after hanging out with her all night and just say goodnight to her at the end instead of making a sexual proposal or gesture.]*

These same men were trying to befriend him so they could get into his inner circle with all these beautiful women, but without any particular success though. The only men he would trust without any second thoughts and allowed them to be around his female companions were his two childhood best friends, Lakis and Tasos.

His popularity had played a significant role in the huge success of his taverna. As a result of this, his biggest desire, dream and ambition was to open multiple tavernas and create a big brand with his name on it. He was thinking for a brand name something like '*Babis Food Heaven*' or '*Eat Like Babis*'.

The second option would make more sense as Babis undoubtedly liked his food and it was his top-level interest. Presentation-wise, he looked like a giant. He was 6ft 5' tall and weighed around thirty stone. The weight especially was a dynamic factor in this equation as he was breaking one personal record after the other about the amount of food he could devour in a day.

His daily food intake was so prodigious that it was a regular source of conflict between him and his mother Soula. To put it in perspective in May 2010, he would routinely finish his day with a feast so epic that it could have put even the most professional eater to shame.

"Maaa... Go and ask Mitso (the grill chef of the taverna) to drop on the charcoal a kilo of lamb chops, one burger stuffed with feta and one pork sausage. I'm starving!" Babis asked Soula, after he crushed on a chair at the table she was sitting.

The time was 1:30am and there was only a group of customers left in the taverna, who were mainly drinking at that point, so the rest of the staff could easily deal with them. Not many minutes before, the kitchen had closed for the customers, but Babis was just starting.

"What?? No! No, no, and no! I'm not! Are you serious now? Is all this food just for you again? My sweet boy... Three people would struggle to finish all this food! I'm not going to help you eat yourself to death. You're already the size of a small house! That's it! No more!" Soula snapped when she heard her son's food order to finish off his night.

"Come on maa... Don't be like that! I'm so exhausted... And I haven't eaten anything since 3pm today! Didn't you see how busy it was tonight? It was one of our best Saturdays ever. The tables didn't stop changing from 8pm until now. I need a bit of food to celebrate it. Come on maa! Ask Mitso to drop the meat on the chargrill. I can't lift my legs now that I sat down. I'm dying..." Babis begged his mother in the same way a junkie asks for change to get some dope.

"So today you want to eat for three people to celebrate this busy Saturday. What was your excuse last night then when you devoured one and a half kilo of lamb chops, two big pork sausages and an omelette topped with feta and chips at 1am? And then, what was all that takeaway food you brought with you when you came back home around 5:30am? In the morning I found on the kitchen table leftovers from a portion of chips with one hundred toppings on them, a small bite left from a double burger and a paper cup with a bit of milkshake in it. You didn't even bother to get rid of them. Were you drinking all night at these bars you go? Are you doing this on purpose to drive me crazy? If you continue like this how any woman will want you? How will any woman find you attractive? How will they want to start a relationship with you if you look like a whale? You have all these pretty girls around you all the time and you never had one of them as a proper girlfriend! Are you only thinking about food? When will you become a father and get me some grandkids? When??"

Babis opened his mouth to answer and before his voice managed to get out of his lips, Soula continued with her rant: "I'm praying to Jesus for you every day. I'm praying to see you with a woman. I'm praying to see grandkids from you. But how will this happen if you continue eating like this? And it's not only for me. No! No! No! Not only for me! It's for you! For your health! The way you eat you'll have problems with diabetes and your heart. Have you forgotten what happened to your father? At least he lived half of his life... But you're still young. It's a shame to destroy your life so early because you eat like a monster! And if something happens to you, then I'll die too. I won't be able to live without you... Without the joy you'll bring me with your beautiful wife and my grandkids! I've lost your father; I can't lose you as well... Promise me you stop eating like this and start exercising from Monday. I'll pay for your gym. And I'll also pay for you to go back to your dietician friend Giannis to help you with a diet. What do you think my sweet little boy?"

"Is this the end of the tape?" Babis asked calmly, but he was burning inside. He then pushed back the chair he was sitting and placed both of his hands on the table to help his massive body stand up. When he was finally standing up, he said peacefully to Soula: "Every night, the same bloody story... When will you finally learn for God's sake mum?"

What he honestly wanted to say to his mum was: *"ihes, then ihes, mas espases ta arhithia". (Είχες, δεν είχες, μας έσπασες τα αρχίδια) [literal translation: You had, you hadn't, you busted our testicles. This phrase is used by Greeks when a person is seriously annoying and puts all the effort in to bust their victim's balls.]* But he decided not to.

Instead, he walked away from the table, went to the kitchen pass and shouted his food order to the grill chef, so Soula could hear it loud and clear from where she was sitting: "Mitso! Drop on the charcoals a kilo of lamb chops, one beef burger stuffed with feta and one pork sausage. Also, get me a grilled feta with honey and two portions of chips with parmesan on top. When ready, put them in takeaway boxes. I'll have them out of here."

He then walked past Soula's table who was still there watching him. The breaking point for her was when her eyes fell on his pyramid shape tits. They were bouncing vigorously under his t-shirt, as they were gaining extra momentum when they were crashing on his swollen tummy.

She waited until he was out of her sight and then ran to the women's toilets. When she was finally there and locked herself inside one of them, she cried like a river.

For everyone and everything in her life.

8:02pm, Thursday 13th May 2010

"Where the bloody hell have you been? Why aren't you at the front like every day? Why are you carrying glasses yourself? Where is the rest of the staff? Why don't you...eh... eh... Oh shit. I forgot what I wanted to say... Why Babis? Why?" asked Tasos intensely, but quietly so the customers wouldn't listen.

"What the hell's wrong with you? Why are you running in here like a maniac? I almost dropped all the glasses on this couple, you malaka! And what's this shit with all the questions? And why you still have your sunglasses on? It's dark out there you idiot!" wondered Babis after he moved like a ballerina to save the tray full of glasses from crushing on the floor. And probably on the couple's heads who were sitting right next to the crash point. This required very sharp reflexes and a movement of his hands at a supersonic speed, which was such an absolute physical challenge for Babis. It was also a spectacular performance for those who had the absolute luck to watch this one-off short show, free of charge from such a close range.

"I'll take these glasses and water to the customers. Just wait at the bar. I'll come and see you there." continued Babis abruptly as he was completely baffled by what had just happened.

"No Babis! I need to speak to you now! I have to... Now!! Tasos exclaimed, visibly overwhelmed and nearly breathless. The sweat was running down his face like he had just completed a full marathon.

"Ok. Listen. Take a deep breath and calm down for a second. Go and sit at a stool at the bar and I'll be there with you as soon as possible. Can you do this for me?" Babis realised that he had to deal with Tasos in a calmer way than usual. He looked like he was way off his head and Babis had no time for any additional drama. His taverna was already on fire!

"Fine…fine, I will do, yes, I will. But don't be late! What I have to say to you can't wait any longer!" said Tasos nodding back to Babis request.

They both left towards opposite directions. Less than a minute later, Babis returned at the bar as he had promised. Tasos was standing up waiting and not sitting on a bar stool as he was asked to do. His foot was tapping out a frantic rhythm as his teeth gnawed at his fingernails in perfect sync.

"Go on then! I am all ears. What happened that is so urgent and I got almost killed by a running malaka like you?" Babis questioned his best friend staring into his sunglasses. "And before you open your mouth, take the stupid sunglasses and this hat off."

Tasos removed both from his steaming head without any objection. Before he spoke again, he checked around if he was being watched by anyone. When he was certain that nobody was looking at them, he said: "I don't know where to start… I really don't." He stopped and drank a sip of water as his mouth had gone Sahara-dessert-style dry. Probably the celebratory mojitos he sipped down less than a couple of hours ago didn't support his body hydration.

"Listen malaka! I don't have all day. And to answer one of the sixty-nine questions you asked me in five seconds, I wasn't at the front like every day because two of my staff called in sick last minute and I'm just left with the sixteen-year-old Fotis, the second assistant to the assistant waiter, to run a crazy busy shift, until Sarantos and Angela come to help me in a bit, so crack on malaka!" Babis lashed out at his mate as he had started losing his patience with him. The taverna and his customers were always his main priority. Always. No matter what.

At least, that's what he thought until that day.

Bondage, fisting, strap-
on and romantic

The historic two-story house stood near the heart of an Athenian suburb, rich with its own storied past. It was built in 1875 and four generations of Babis' family have lived in it. Its two floors and spacious yard at the front, had been very well preserved for over a century by almost all the generations of this family.

Until the Second World War, Babis' family had always been upper-middle class. His grandfather and great-grandfather had been amongst the main contractors the Greek government was using to complete big public projects. Their main area of expertise was the construction of big roads and main highways in the Metropolitan area of Athens and the province of Attiki.

But they also had another very strong area of expertise: bribing public officials. They bribed them to be appointed with the construction projects and bribed them again when they were supposed to deliver the completed projects.

In Greece, the construction industry had a long and storied history of bribery. Construction companies, like the one belonged to Babis' family, have perfected the art of greasing the palms of public officials to get their projects approved, even if they're only half-finished or not meeting the technical specifications to the letter. This industry was so entrenched that it had been going strong since modern Greece was founded as a country in the 19th century.

The practice of bribery was widespread and a common secret within the wider Greek society. Many Greeks frequently discussed allegations of construction companies paying bribes to public officials to secure contracts get their projects approved, expedite the permitting process and get them to look the other way when they're cutting corners on the agreed specifications of the construction projects.

The Second World War had brought Greece to its knees. After the end of WWII, the country was starved, beaten and broken. Its people were traumatized, the infrastructure was in ruins and the economy in shambles. At this low point in the country's history, the Greeks did what they seemed to enjoy most and were extremely competent at: they turned on each other and started a civil war. This would tear the country apart and leave it even more traumatized than it already was.

To provide some context, imagine Greece inside a knackered and filthy human body. What was happening was that the left hand, the military branch of the Communist Party of Greece was fighting the right hand, the Hellenic Army of the Greek government, and vice versa. Greece was slapping its own grubby and decaying face with both of its own hands in turns. They fought for five years and in the end, the government's side won. As a direct result, the Greek people were plunged into a living nightmare of extreme poverty and misery. The majority of the Athenians were hit hardest, as their urban lifestyle left them with few self-sustainable options.

But this wasn't the case for Babis' family. They had accumulated a great amount of wealth, mainly in the form of property and land. All those semi-completed, lacking in quality projects and the bribing party they held with the Greek authorities all the years before the Second World War, proved to be invaluable in that critical moment in time.

It wasn't long until the third-generation rule' came into play for them. According to this rule, most families will lose their wealth when they reach their third generation. Or as the

Greeks say in such cases, *'opios katurai sti thalasa, to vriski sto alati tu'. (Όποιος κατουράει στη θάλασσα το βρίσκει στο αλάτι του). [literal translation: Whoever urinates in the sea, he will find it in his salt. This phrase is used for those who do bad things and at some point, life repays them in a similar nasty way.]*

This family hit the jackpot with Ilias, Babis' father, who was the third generation in it. Ilias' values and life theory was the exact opposite to those his father and grandfather held.

Babis' grandfather had given his best to get his wife pregnant, but they had a series of unsuccessful attempts, including two miscarriages. But with intense prayers to Jesus, regular visits to any monastery available, which came with generous donations from the wealthy family, the miracle happened.

In April 1945, Jesus finally decided to change his mind and sent them little Ilias as a present. This happened at the end of the Second World War and despite the harsh living conditions in the society around him, he was raised like a proper royal. Since he was the only child in this wealthy family, he developed to a spoilt little prick. He had anything he desired, including the most expensive clothes and toys, and was always fed with the most premium food. He would rarely hear the word 'no' from his parents, especially his mother.

After he became an adult, only externally as he was just an oversized toddler, he used his peanut-size brain to continue living the big life regardless of any consequences. He was out every night gambling, drinking in night clubs and having expensive affairs with different short-term 'girlfriends'.

He was completely uncontrollable and his father, who was the only person in the family who might had a chance to change all this, became ill and grew fairly weak, making it difficult for him to set any boundaries on his one and only child. Anyway, it was already too late for something like this to happen. He had officially become a spoilt, skill-less, arrogant, money wasting animal.

It didn't take long for the family's wealth to be minimised

to a critical level by Ilias and his luxurious life. So, around the end of 1970's, only a handful of properties were still owned by the family, including this family house, which was a shadow of its previous glory.

Ilias couldn't care less about maintaining this building. He was always busy spending his hardworking ancestors' wealth like there's no tomorrow. It was only after he was married to Soula in January 1977, when he finally began thinking a bit more responsibly and realised that he had to maintain the house to a decent condition for his own future family to live in it.

But their finances had been brought down to their knees and the former glorious spending-money-like-crazy days were long gone. He and his fifteen years younger wife, Soula, were working now as civil servants in low skilled positions, after a local MP planted them there, paying back Ilias and his family a favour for supporting him in the national elections for years.

This was so very common in Greece that it even has a name; it's called 'Rousfeti': The Greek Art of Bribery.

This poetic and sinister term comes from the Turkish word 'rüşvet' which means bribery. It specifically refers to the practice of exchanging favours between voters and politicians. In essence, it was a form of mutual bribery, with each side giving something to the other to get what they want. For voters, rousfeti could take the form of a job, a promotion, or even just a promise of future help of any type. For politicians, it could mean votes, campaign contributions, or even just the knowledge that they had the support of a powerful individual and their social circle.

Rousfeti was a deeply ingrained part of Greek culture and had a profound impact on the country's political system. It had led to corruption, nepotism and a general distrust of all governments. It had also damaged the economy, as it had led to the hiring of completely useless and unqualified officials and the awarding of contracts to cronies. Rousfeti, being a highly corrosive force that undermined democracy and economic growth for decades, had contributed massively to economic and social decline Greece was experiencing.

As a result of the lack of maintenance and care, this great building was deteriorating to such an extent that it was no longer habitable. In October 1978, Ilias and young Soula had to move to an apartment in the town centre, which also belonged to the family.

In 1999 Ilias died from a heart attack. He was only fifty-four years old, and it came as a huge shock to everyone as he was on top of his medication and the guidance received from his cardiologist.

 It was little Babis who inherited the old family house. But he had to wait until he was eighteen years old to be legally able to make any decisions about the building and its future. This meant that he had a lot of time to think what the best option for him and this historic structure was.

Babis was addicted to food from a very young age. He was spending hours and hours thinking about it, learning how to cook it and then eating it. This boy was deeply influenced by his parents' main and sometimes only topic of discussion: *'What are we going to eat?'*

A lengthy discussion between Ilias and Soula usually started by one of them asking the other any of the following:

What are we eating tomorrow?

Where are we buying the X ingredients for the Y recipe?

Who has the best prices for the X?

Who's the best butcher for lamb?

Who's the best butcher for pork?

Who's the best butcher for chicken?

Which greengrocer has the best vegetables and fruits?

What time are we collecting the food we sent to the local bakery to cook in their oven?

And the list went on...

Everything was based around how they were going to fill their stomachs to the max and reach ultimate happiness by devouring anything edible. Their diet included several extreme options like pigeons with tomato sauce and spaghetti in the oven, lamb's brain salad with olive oil, lemon and chopped red onions and finally, the chicken legs and combs boiled in a soup with rice.

Babis was fifteen years old when he first dreamt of owning his own restaurant. He would often go to the family house alone and imagine how he would transform it into a beautiful and inviting dining space. He would picture the tables set with white linens, the smell of freshly grilled lamb chops wafting through the air and the sound of laughter and conversations filling the room. And him in the centre of the restaurant, like a maestro conducting his staff harmonically, offering ultimate satisfaction to all his guests.

As he got older, his dream only grew stronger and when he finally turned eighteen, he officially started the process of turning the family house into a taverna.

Reality struck him pretty soon though and he realised that this was a hell of a project for him. He had to organise everything about the taverna including equipment, food costing, operating procedures, menus, suppliers, interior design, marketing and promotions, and the list went on... It was impossible to put all the above together by himself as he had no clue about most of these areas. He had no choice but to propose to his older brother, Vasilis, to become his business partner and support him in all these unbelievably complicated areas.

Vasilis got involved straight away with the authorities and specifically with the planning permission required to start the taverna business. He soon found out that they had to deal with an extremely complicated issue with the construction of the building.

When this house was built in 1875, the planning of the town and its streets were designed to cover the citizens' transportation needs of that period. The main means of transport then were animals like donkeys and horses, and also horse-drawn carriages. The streets were narrow and you had to be quite lucky to find a straight road for longer than sixty feet as they all went around the anarchically built houses.

The local politicians were doing favours in the form of *rousfeti* to the locals so they could get their extended family's votes. When a new road was supposed to be constructed and required parts of houses or even entire buildings to be demolished, the crooked Greek politicians were getting into business. They would allow their future voters to keep their houses intact and the new road had to be constructed around their building, regardless of the civil engineers' planning. The result was an eyesore, but in reality, nobody seemed to care as long as the politicians were elected and the voters kept their houses intact.

This way of constructing the inner-city road network continued for decades after decades. The Greeks would rarely elect visionary politicians, who were bold enough to implement a normal plan for the urban road network and disregard several citizens' demands to keep their properties untouched. In summary, *'otan ton kolo vazis mayira, skata tha mayirepsi'. (όταν τον κώλο βάζεις μάγειρα, σκατά θα μαγειρέψει) [literal translation: When you appoint the ass as a chef, he will cook shit. This is used when the wrong people are appointed in the wrong positions and bring the wrong results. Such a great match for most of the Greek politicians.]*

After the 1970-80s, the road network planning of the towns had massively changed, reflecting the people's current transportation methods, compared to those over one hundred years ago. This was creating a massive complication for Babis and his dreams of becoming a taverna owner.

A small part of it was supposed to be used for a new wider street and for this reason, it had to be demolished. The family was well connected with the officials from the local city council for decades, mainly through the bribing party they held with them. Consequently, the officials had turned a blind eye to this 'extremely minor – almost non-existent - issue', based on the fact that nobody from the family ever tried to change the usage of the building to something different than a residential property.

Babis and Vasilis couldn't start operating their restaurant business, until they managed to find a solution without having to demolish any part of the building. Otherwise, bye-bye taverna for now.

Vasilis was referred by Nikolas, a very powerful and deeply connected neighbour, to Giota, a civil engineer who had a close relationship with Vaggelis, the director of the urban planning authority. Nikolas reassured him that she could find an easy and fast solution to this *'so small / not so significant / nobody is genuinely affected by it'* issue.

Vasilis had arranged a meeting between him, Babis and Giota to discuss the options available, in order to override this critical issue. The meeting was scheduled at the taverna on a Saturday morning for 11:30am.

The night before, Vasilis stayed out until late and consumed a considerable amount of alcohol. He decided to finish the night with some pork kebabs from a different takeaway than the regular one he was using on such occasions. His choice didn't prove to be a fortunate one. He suffered from a serious food poisoning with severe diarrhoea and vomiting, which kept him up for the rest of the night. In combination with the hangover from the booze, he was one step before being admitted to the hospital and, definitely, in no position to attend this serious meeting in the morning.

At 9:45am, almost an hour before the meeting, he informed Babis that he would have to go solo on this occasion and asked him to say to Giota that he was sick with serious gastroenteritis. Babis didn't take this easily and got extremely anxious for this meeting. But he had no choice but to be there all by himself.

Vasilis then called Giota and apologised for not being able to attend their meeting. He lied to her by saying that he contracted gastroenteritis as he didn't want to come across as irresponsible and careless with the way he's conducting business. He explained that his brother Babis would be there. And that he was more than capable to understand what she would ask them to do.

Babis was sitting at a table waiting for Giota to arrive. Inside the taverna all the tables and chairs were set up like it was opening that same evening. Everything was ready for the business to start serving customers, only one small detail was missing: the planning permission for the change of usage of this building to a taverna.

In a normal country where the laws were working as expected, this permission would be the first thing they needed to obtain to be allowed to carry out any works. But in Greece, things didn't work this way, if you knew the shortcuts and the right people. So, Babis and Vasilis had completed all the required construction works and repairs on the building before they were even granted the planning permission to do so.

The time was already 11am and Babis was frantically biting his nails.

"The malaka Vasilis.

Found the day to be sick.

What the hell do I say to her now?

I have no clue about planning shit and permissions and shit like that.

I don't think I'll understand half of what she says to me...

Why didn't he rearrange this stupid meeting?

The malaka!

Every time, the same shit with him..." he thought while his anxiety was so high that he could taste it.

The main door opened and Giota entered the room. When Babis saw her, he shot up from his chair like a rocket, nearly sending the table and all its contents flying. Giota walked until she reached the table he was waiting.

"Hi." she greeted him without any facial expression and sat down.

"Hello! How are you today? Did it take you long to park? Was it easy to find our place?" replied Babis trying to hide his nervousness by making an attempt for small talk.

"What happened to your brother?" answered Giota and dismissed all his questions with a cold stare.

"Oh! My brother! He's not well. He has gastereon... ehm... gastoroe... gestoraent... ehm... gaestroanter... Ooooh! Screw this! He has the runs and he says he's very sorry he can't be here today." replied Babis, who was so pissed off with himself that he could easily karate-chop the table in front of him in half.

"Ok." she replied with an icy expression.

Babis ran at the bar and brought one bottle of an ice-cold Greek beer. He shared it between the two beer glasses which were already on their table as if they were waiting for this meeting to happen for a long time.

"Vaggelis has a very contrarian spirit and a rather mercurial temperament. I understand that you and your brother must already be aware of this." explained Giota with the look of a fox.

"What the hell!

She started speaking Chinese...

What's this thing she just said now?" he thought.

"You mean he's a malaka? I know this Giota. I have a friend and he's trying to open his restaurant for a year and he's getting screwed all the time by this Vaggelis and every time he tries to speak with this him, 99% he is not available and when he finds him, this Vaggelis finds a new problem and asks for another document and this document is impossible to get and my friend has to start again. I don't understand what is going on and we can't be screwed like this to be honest." Babis ranted on about what he was facing.

"This is unsurprising, given the current state of affairs in the Greek public services." she replied and took a good sip from her freezing glass filled with beer.

"For God's sake!

What this 'current state of a fur' is?

Do they skin animals in the stupid public services now?

Is she saying all this shit on purpose to ask for more money at the end?

She wants to confuse me the bitch!" he thought again and looked at Giota like a deer in the headlights.

"But there is always a way around to get your job done and open the taverna." said Giota who had been dealing with similar cases in the local public services for over twenty-five years.

"What is it? Do you know it? asked Babis praying only for a positive answer.

"I think I do. It all depends on you. And how far you're willing to go." replied Giota using a very stable tone of voice. Then she took another good sip of the cold beer.

"So? What is it? Tell me! Please! We're in the shit with Vasilis. We're four months behind schedule and we want to open before this Christmas and I think we won't because of that stupid corner of the building. And Vasilis said, if we have to knock it down, we're screwed and that it will cost us extra tens of thousands of Euros that we don't have. Please tell me what we need to do Giota..." said Babis and his eyes were brimming with desperation, like a lost three-year-old boy at a crowded Christmas fair.

"I am fully apprised of the facts of your case, as your brother has already provided me with a comprehensive overview." replied Giota.

"Ooooh!

Here she goes again with the Chinese.

What's wrong with her?

Why she doesn't speak Greek like a normal person?" wondered Babis silently inside his head, still looking at her desperately, waiting for the magical remedy to their problem.

"Ok then. Listen carefully now. What I will say to you, needs to stay here. Full confidentiality. If it goes out, apart from the fact that I'll deny everything and sue the life out of you for defamation, I'll make sure that you will never get this planning permission. To put it in simple words, if you say anything, you're done. Big time, proper done. Are you ok to go ahead under these conditions?" asked Giota with the same cold, steady and unemotional voice, sounding like she had said the same exact thing numerous times before. And then she had another sip of the cold beer.

"Yes! Yes! I am ok with this! What you say stays here with me. You have my word!" Babis pleaded her to trust him with her magical solution. All this time, he hadn't touched his beer. He was only holding the beer glass firmly with both of his hands, looking directly at Giota's lips.

"Ok then. Listen carefully. Vaggelis needs to be paid two and a half thousand euro to sign the planning permission."

"What?? Is that all? Are you joking? Is that all?" Babis was so surprised he couldn't believe it was finally so simple. "That's not a problem at all! I'll get him the money tomorrow!" he continued totally excited that his problem was about to be resolved in such a simple and fast manner.

"I haven't finished yet." said Giota and had another sip of the cold beer.

"Oh shit...What else now?" asked Babis in terror, sweating from fear of what he would hear coming out of her red juicy lips now.

"You need to prepare a DVD with porn for him." replied Giota with her steady blasé voice like she said the most normal thing in the world.

"What?? What?? What did you just say??" asked Babis completely baffled as he couldn't process what he just heard. He basically thought that he misheard what she just said. At least he hoped so...

"And the porn in the DVD can't be of your choice. I'll give you a specific list of categories you must include in it. Strictly nothing out of these categories." explained Giota using the same steady, lacking any excitement and nerve in her tone of voice. She then had another sip of the cold beer.

"I'm sorry... Are you joking now? Is this one of my brother's pranks? Vasilis are you here?" he shouted and started looking around, expecting his brother to appear from where he was hiding all this time.

"Let me dispel any misconceptions you may have. I am here to assist you as a matter of personal obligation to Nikolas. This is the sole reason. Trust me on it. So. Tell me now if you can do it or not. I cannot afford to waste any more time." Giota changed her tone of voice now. She sent him a warning showing that she wasn't messing around and could just leave him in the absolute shit if he wouldn't take her seriously. Then she finished the remaining beer from her glass.

Babis didn't have much of a choice at that point. He had to ignore the fact that this was an unbelievably ridiculous and completely unexpected request. If he wanted to be able to go ahead with the taverna, he should get serious with it. So now, he had to find out the technicalities of the request.

"Ok. Ok. What he wants in it then?" he asked her seriously.

"Bondage, fisting, strap-on and romantic." replied Giota in a completely professional manner like she was presenting a project to a business meeting with the board of directors and the key stakeholders.

"And romantic?? I'm gonna lose my head today!! What romantic has to do with the other three? You know what? Just screw it. I'll stop asking now. I'll just do what I need to do. It's already too much for my head..." exclaimed Babis while he tried to come in terms with what he had just heard.

"Please inform me when you have completed your preparations with the DVD and I will promptly deliver it to him. The sooner you are able to do so, the better it will be for you and your taverna." said Giota and made a pause. "To conclude, the most important part is this."

"There's more? Tell me now that I also have to be the main actor in all the porn videos as well..." he commented, laughing sarcastically and preparing for the worst now.

"With Vaggelis, it works in two stages. Stage one. You give me the DVD and then I give it to him to check it. Only if he approves it, he will go ahead at stage two. This is where you pay him the money and he signs the planning permission. If he doesn't approve it, you get one more chance. If you are unsuccessful the second time as well, then you're out. Meaning, no taverna for you soon my darling." Giota explained in her steady monotone, with her face wearing in the same mask of indifference.

"Why couldn't this Vaggelis be like the all the other civil servants who just give you a price, nice and simple, and then get their *'fakelaki'*? *(φακελάκι) [literal translation: little envelope. This term is commonly used in Greece to describe a bribe.]* How hard it is now to create a DVD with the 'Best of bondage, fisting, strap-on and romantic porn' for this crazy Vaggelis? And what the hell romantic has to do with the other categories??" Babis could continue with his questions until the 32nd of August, but Giota cut him off.

"Call me when you're ready. Bye." she said. She got up, took her purse, put on her sunglasses and walked out of the main entrance of the taverna.

Babis was left there staring at Giota's back while she was walking away. He was still holding the beer glass with both of his massive hands. He still couldn't believe what he had just experienced. His highest hope now was that Vasilis would jump out of a corner and shout: *'Got you malaka!'*

This never happened.

And that's when he felt extremely tense. In his brain, a Greek phrase was on repeat: *'opios pithai pola palukia, to ena beni ston kolo tu'. (Όποιος πηδάει πολλά παλούκια, το ένα μπαίνει στον κώλο του.) [literal translation: Whoever tries to jump over many stakes, one of them will end up in his ass. This phrase is used when someone tries to complete a lot of risky tasks simultaneously and describes the possibility of a dramatic failure in one of them.]*

His experience around porn was pretty basic. Therefore, he knew very well that he lacked the competency to successfully complete the project 'Best of bondage, fisting, strap-on and romantic porn for malaka Vaggelis'. Especially in a level of quality that would satisfy the most perverted and corrupt Greek public official he had ever heard of.

Giota gave him a very clear warning: if he opened his mouth to anyone about it, he would be totally destroyed by her. And he totally agreed with it.

So, what was the very first thing Babis decided to do then? A couple of minutes after she left, he picked up the phone and called his best mate Tasos.

"Malaka, I need massive help. I'm in big shit right now."

"What happened? asked Tasos.

"Swear to your abs that you won't ask me why I need what I'll ask you." said Babis in a very serious manner.

"You know I can't mess with my abs, you prick!" replied Tasos with a soft laughter.

"Listen to me! It'll make no difference to you if you don't know why I need what I'm going to ask you to do for me. Do you understand malaka?" he shouted at Tasos totally pissed off. He was ready to give hell to his mate if he said anything but 'Yes, I swear.'

"Ok, I swear. Tell me now what you need to see how I can help you. Malaka, eh malaka!" replied Tasos.

"I need a DVD with high quality bondage, fisting, strap-on and romantic porn in it." said Babis reluctantly, waiting for

Tasos to burst out laughing with his bizarre request.

"Let me take a wild guess... Is it for the director of the urban planning authority, Vaggelis the Perv?"

"What?? What?? What the hell malaka?!!" Babis was caught by absolute surprise. He couldn't believe that Tasos knew the reason he wanted this DVD. He was completely thunderstruck. "How the bloody hell you know about it? Are you and Vasilis playing me? Are you pricks?" he shouted at Tasos as he still believed deep inside him that this was one of his brother's pranks he had experienced in the past.

"What? Cut the bullshit. This is a real thing. Listen to me carefully my malaka now! You just hit the jack pot! I've made a new friend from the gym, even though he's a bit of a weirdo. He was telling me the other day about this exact thing. He's a geek with computers and IT. Kind of a hacker basically. So, through some of his connections, he was sent several people in the last year, who were asking him to create a DVD with high quality bondage, fisting, strap-on and romantic porn in it. Nobody gave him an explanation about it. Only one of them did and explained who the DVD was for." replied Tasos as seriously as he could.

"Unbelievable... And is he any good at it? Did this pervert bastard like them? Did they pass the first round? "asked Babis wishing only for a 'yes' to each of his questions.

"As far as I know, from what he told me, he has 100% success so far. No same person asked him to do a second one." replied Tasos.

"My man! My man! How can you ask him to do one for me then? "asked Babis excitedly with his eyes wide open and his heart racing as he seriously felt that opening his taverna could happen sooner than he thought.

"He's charging three hundred euro for this shit, so you know. Are you happy to pay all this money just for a stupid DVD?"

"Are you a malaka??" Babis screamed. "Of course I'm happy to pay three hundred euro!" he then exclaimed with a high voice and continued: "I'm already exhausted and we haven't even finished with the rest of the authorities yet. I knew that we needed to bribe all the corrupted assholes in there, but I didn't expect anything like this. I know this is Greece, but this is some next level shit. By the way, how's this pervert Vaggelis still a director and no one has touched him? Do you know?"

"His sister is married with Papadakis, the local MP." replied Tasos.

"Ok. Stop there. Say no more." said Babis and shook his head.

The DVD was, as promised, successful at the first round. Babis got his planning permission signed within the same week. His dream of becoming a taverna owner was about to come true.

With the official stamp from the Greek authorities.

8:09pm, Thursday 13th May 2010

During their spectacular crash, Babis and Tasos were being monitored and recorded by the taverna's high-quality, super-efficient and never-malfunctioning CCTV system: Babis' mother, Soula. An eagle-eyed woman, never missing a detail in front of her eyes and always wanting to know everything. From the taverna troubles to personal issues, anything non-of-her-business.

The problem these two had was that Soula was sitting in a table with two of her friends and had watched everything from the beginning, when Tasos entered the taverna like a lunatic with his baseball cup and sunglasses on. This meant one thing; she already had one million questions to be answered. Soula knew Tasos since he was born as he was the same age and best friends with her second son Babis. They all had lived in the same neighbourhood for all these years as well.

"Will you tell me what happened? Come on malaka! Go on! Or you want me to come back in a few minutes when you ready to speak?" Babis was losing his patience with his best friend.

He was seriously thinking of leaving him for a bit to go and help with the service, as the taverna was incredibly busy with almost no staff available. Standing there like two idiots having a chat while his business was on fire and Soula watching every move they made from head to toe, wasn't a very smart choice to make.

Tasos moved closer to Babis' right ear and whispered: "We had sex man! We had sex! I can't believe it... I honestly can't! It happened out of nowhere... I was not prepared at all! I still can't believe it! I don't know how it happened. We had sex at the park and at the end she gave me a blowjob and I came all over my pants and they're fully covered in cum now and I'm meeting with them and my family in thirty minutes here and my pants look like shit now... Help me please! I have no

31

clue what to do..."

"Shut up malaka and follow me to the toilets now. Don't say another word." Babis almost dragged his best mate into the toilets.

He completed a fast check that nobody was in there so they could speak freely. Check completed, toilets clear. He then turned to Tasos and asked: "Who did you have sex with?"

"With Barbara..." replied Tasos.

"What?? Say again. With who??" Babis couldn't believe in his ears.

"With Barbara. Barbara..." Tasos replied with a shaking voice and his head facing the toilet floor like he was ready to say his last prayer.

"Look at me now malaka!" Babis raised his voice just at the right level so the sound could not escape the small toilet space. "Lakis' mum and Lupo's wife?? This Barbara you mean?"

"Yes..." Tasos replied.

"I can't believe it! Are you stupid or what? Just tell me you're messing with me now. Come on malaka! Say it!"

"No, I'm not." replied Tasos.

"I can't believe you! She's Lakis' mum you son of a bitch! And what the hell? You dared to touch Lupo's wife??? Are you a malaka? Oh my God..." wondered Babis, looking straight into Tasos' eyes and holding both of his shoulders down to the ground as if Tasos was ready to take off and disappear forever. "If you wanted to stick your stupid willy in a hole, why didn't you go to the brothels like always, you big fat malaka?"

A simple please... If that's
ok with you Madam...

Tasos, Lakis and Babis were at the playground in the local park, sitting on a swing each, with their bikes left lying on the ground around them. It was a sunny Friday in early June 2003, with temperatures reaching 29°C (84.2°F) and the school year coming to an end soon. This was their usual meeting place after school, until they had to go back home, usually around 2:30pm, to have lunch with their families.

"I can't wait for tomorrow! I can't! I can't!" shouted Tasos excitedly.

"I'm not very sure about it." said Babis with the opposite tone in his voice, nowhere near to Tasos' excitement.

"Me too. Maybe we leave it for another time. Now that I think again about it, I feel I'm not quite ready as well..." added Lakis, supporting Babis' hesitation.

"Come on you two! Didn't we discuss about it a hundred times already? You both agreed. So, why you change your mind last minute?" asked Tasos showing his disappointment to both of his best friends.

"I don't know..." Lakis responded.

"Me too..." followed Babis.

"Ok, ok, I get it. We're just fifteen years old and you both feel it's a bit early for it. But you know very well that almost all the other boys in our class say that they have already been to the brothels. We're almost the last ones left who are still virgins. Do you want the other boys to spread rumours around the school that we are faggots? Like they already did with Mihalis and Stefanos?" Tasos used all his heavy armour to persuade them to go ahead with their visit to the 'girls'.

"No! No! Never! I wouldn't be able to live with such a shame!" answered Lakis showing that he became upset with this scenario.

"Me too! Me too!" added Babis and continued: "Nobody calls us faggots! Never!"

"Now that I think about it, what happens if we meet someone we know on our way to the brothels and asks us where we go? There's nothing else we could go towards that way. We all need to say the same story." noticed Lakis very seriously, still showing strong signs of hesitation.

"Yes! What we'll say Tasos? What?" followed Babis echoing Lakis.

"I have thought of this too my men! We'll say that we're going to my uncle Stavros' garage to spend some hours there to see how he fixes the cars. The garage is almost next to the brothels and we all love cars boys! Am I freaking smart or what?" Tasos boasted to his mates with a feeling of superiority and enormous self-confidence. He then performed a victory dance as if he had scored a goal for his team during the national school football championship final, on the 93rd minute, when the score was 3-3.

"Yes, but what will happen then if your uncle Stavros sees us passing from his garage? Have you even thought about it? asked Lakis again, trying to cover any potential angle of the story that could go wrong. His lack of excitement was somewhat obvious even to the untrained eyes.

"Yes Tasos! What will happen then? Whaaat??" followed Babis just milliseconds after Lakis completed his point. Babis was experiencing frequent voice breaks as he transitioned from a boy to a man during his teenage years. The first question was made in a deep manly voice, but the second one, the 'Whaaat?', sounded like a turkey warning the other turkeys in the team that Christmas is coming.

"You know my uncle had a surgery on Monday, I told you we visited him at the hospital with my mum. So, there's no way on earth to see us passing from his garage tomorrow." explained Tasos a bit more intensely now. He paused for two seconds and then he asked them, remarkably frustrated now:

"Are we all happy now? Do we all have the same story in our heads or not? God's sake..."

"But Tasos... If this person we meet who knows us, also knows that your uncle had a surgery. What do we say then?" asked Lakis again.

"We say that my uncle's assistant will be there and shows us how they fix the cars. Ok now?" replied Tasos.

"And what if we get AIDS or any othe..." Babis tried to ask one more reasonable question, but he was cut off abruptly by Tasos.

"But what about this Tasos, what about the other Tasos, you have busted my balls you two little sissies with all your questions! You know what? We have the perfect plan. And none of all these things you asked me will ever happen. And if they happen, we have my plan. So, both of you stop acting like babies! Man up and let's get ready for our big day. We're going to the brothels tomorrow laaaaaaads!!" shouted Tasos and moved towards his two best friends, giving both a strong hug.

While they were both body-locked by Tasos' hug, Lakis looked Babis into his eyes in despair and Babis shook his head in agreement. But they're both going to the brothels on Saturday, that was indisputable.

After the big group hug, they all got on their bikes and rode away from the playground to return to their homes for the family lunch.

On Saturday, at 10:30 am, Lakis and Babis arrived at the playground on their bikes, following the plan. Tasos was already there, waiting for them. He's sitting on one of the swings, with his sunglasses and a baseball cap on. When he saw them approaching, he shouted with enormous excitement: "Laaaaaaads!!" He then stood up and ran towards them.

"I haven't slept at all last night, but I don't give a shit! I'm ready to have sex like a beast!" he announced to his two best friends and continued: "The day has come! I can't believe it! The day has come booooyys!". He was so hyper as if he had added a cocktail of cocaine and speed in the milk with cornflakes he had for breakfast.

"Are we ready? And I say... Are we ready boys?" he roared at both Lakis and Babis. At the same time, he was shaking them as he had grabbed them both from their shoulders. He was trying to light a fire under their asses, as their level of excitement wasn't matching this 'big day'. They were both standing like two condemned men in the death row, silent and still, awaiting to be executed on the electric chair.

"Yes. We are." replied Lakis silently, while he was still being squeezed by Tasos vigorous hug.

"Yes." followed Babis demonstrating the same level of excitement he would have, if he was just informed that he was sentenced to work at a Russian gulag for the rest of his life.

Tasos didn't pay much attention to his mates' vibes. All he cared for was to lose his virginity as a matter of highest urgency.

Without any further ado, they got on their bikes and left from the playground where they had spent hours and hours playing together since they remembered themselves. The bike ride should take them approximately twenty minutes as the brothels were located in the outskirts of the town. So, they should be there by 11am. Tasos was very strict with the timeline of his 'genius' plan and didn't want to miss a beat. Therefore, he was heading the bicycle convoy to its sacred journey to the loss of virginity and start of manhood. He was cycling like a maniac, leaving the other two, who were trying to keep up with his ridiculously fast pace, far behind.

After sixteen minutes of exhausting bike riding, they finally arrived at the bordellos. There were four different little detached bungalows, two in each side of the plot, which was almost in the middle of nowhere. Just some garages and warehouses were nearby, but nothing right next to this 'plot of sin'. Usually, there were several cars parked inside the car park next to the houses, but since it was Saturday morning, it was dead. This meant that the boys would be the first customers of a busy like always Saturday.

They stopped about sixty feet away from the first house, where the cars usually parked. They wanted to complete the final 'losing our virginity' arrangements.

Before Tasos managed to let any syllables out of his mouth, Lakis dropped his bike and ran towards a tree. When he reached it, he leaned on it with both hands and vomited.

"What's that all about now??" wondered Tasos. This wasn't included in his super-genius agenda for this extra-special day.

"What's... that... all about?... I'll tell you... now.... what's... that all about..." responded Babis who's sweating and completely out of breath from the lunatic bike ride. He then added angrily: "You rode your bike... like a lion was chasing you... malaka... and we couldn't keep up with you... Couldn't you look... behind?... Lakis is vomiting... because of you... because you want to have sex... like crazy... you big fat... malaka!"

"Yes, I understand, but..." Tasos tried to answer, but Babis was so pissed off that he didn't let him finish his excuse and shouted at him: "But... Go screw yourself you idiot!"

"That's why we're here anyway, aren't we?" Tasos replied jokingly to his annoyed friend in a miserable attempt to change his mood.

Lakis finally went back to his friends looking like death warmed over, with a pale and sweaty face. His t-shirt was partially covered in vomit, stinking even from a few feet away.

"I'm not going in there today... I don't feel very well... I'll wait for you here. You can go..." mumbled Lakis, looking down at the ground.

"What? Say again Lakis. I couldn't hear a word of what you just said." replied Tasos.

"I'm not going in there! You go! Ok?" Lakis screamed back at Tasos looking angrily straight into his eyes, with a bit of vomit still dripping from his chin.

"Ok, ok, ok, no problem. I get it my mate, I get it. You wait here. Take your time and relax. We'll be back soon." Tasos suggested gently to his worn-out friend.

He then turned towards Babis. "I'm going in the first house on the left. There's a blonde babe in there and they told me she's out of this world! She's very thin, with small tits and a crazy round ass! I can't wait to stick it in her! I believe you like big and brunette more, so you go to the first one on the right. They told me there's a tall brunette with long hair and massive tits in that one. She'll drain all your juices! You'll come out of there looking like a raisin!"

He tapped Babis twice on the back, grabbed him under his left arm and walked with him towards the four houses with the red light on, indicating that they were open for business.

"I'm a bit stressed. Still not sure about it..." said Babis just before they split in different directions with Tasos.

"Listen. You'll go in there and you'll smash her! She'll beg you to stop! Trust me! Let's go tiger! This is your time!" Tasos encouraged his hesitant friend and extended his fist confidently, anticipating Babis' fist to meet his back with equal energy. In return, Babis reluctantly stretched his fist and touched Tasos with deafening silence.

When Babis entered the first house on the right, he came across a very short, skinny, old woman, in her mid-seventies, sitting in an armchair, smoking a cigarette and reading a newspaper. When she saw him coming in, she left the newspaper on the side table next to her and scanned him with her eyes from head to toe. Then without saying a word to him, she left that room and entered another room through an internal door, still holding her cigarette.

He was left standing there, not knowing what to do exactly, so he looked around in the room. This was the customer waiting-area, for when the bordello was busy, with three armchairs on one side and a big sofa on the other. Even though it was almost midday on a very sunny day, the windows were sealed and no light was allowed inside. The room was lit with a number of blue and red coloured lights at various spots, all dimmed very low to create a dark and erotic atmosphere. An incense stick was burning on a little side table, emitting a sensual fragrance and its exotic scent was filling the air. The walls were all painted in a deep purple colour, with loads of different shaped mirrors hanging on them.

The old woman returned to the room. She looked at Babis and, without any intention for a small talk, said with her gravelly voice: "Blowjob or wank forty Euro. Simple sixty. In the ass eighty. All included, special price, a hundred. What you want?"

"Hmmmm....eeeee......hmmmm..." came out of Babis mouth as he experienced a sudden brain freeze.

"Listen little boy. It's getting dark outside and your mummy will be looking for you. You need to decide today. The big men will be here soon. What you wanna to do with Nicole?" asked the madam of the house with her rough voice, who was already getting frustrated with Babis' indecisiveness.

"A simple please... If that's ok with you Miss... "replied Babis ready to break into two massive pieces.

"Do I look like a Miss to you? You only call me Madam. Ok?" answered the woman abruptly.

"A simple please... If that's ok with you Madam..." replied Babis with the correct title for her now. His stress automatically reached the maximum limit. His whole body sweated like he was inside a hammam, so intensely that he could even feel his sweat dripping from his back down to his ass.

"Ok. Sixty." said the madam. She then stretched her right arm, opened her palm and waited for Babis to pay her. He took the money out of his back pocket and pass it to her. His sweat had made the three twenty-euro paper notes quite soggy.

"What's this boy? Did you just take them out of your ass?

Do they smell like shit too? Jeeesus... Follow me." said the madam with a sour face and walked towards the room she had previously been in. She was still smoking her cigarette.

"This is Nicole. She'll give you a simple. Behave well. Don't do any shit to her. I'm outside." the madam warned Babis and disappeared like a midget ninja out of there.

"Come over here my love! What's your name?" asked Nicole with a deep sexual voice, lying on a big double bed in the middle of the room. The atmosphere in there was similar to the waiting room, just a bit darker.

"Babis." he replied without being able to tell how Nicole looked like as he could barely see her from where he was standing.

"I love your name Babis! It's so masculine!" she replied. She then stood up from the bed and walked towards him. After a couple of steps, he could finally see her clearly.

Nicole was a very tall woman in her mid-fifties, almost 6ft 5' tall with long black hair and a very thick red lipstick on her face, which made her look like a bullfrog. She was wearing a see-through kimono, like a fish net, allowing every part of her gigantic body to be 100% visible. She had a massive pair of breasts with the nipples looking sadly towards the floor and an extremely hairy vagina. One could easily smuggle a small pouch full of diamonds through the borders by hiding it inside this glorious bush.

"Come here with me, you sexy boy!" she said to Babis and grabbed his left hand. She walked with him until they reached the bed.

"Now, take of your clothes. I'm so crazy for you! I want you sexy boy!" she said, dropping the fish-net-kimono she was wearing and going fully naked.

"Shit...

I need to take my clothes off too.

What am I doing in here?" Babis wondered.

He managed to take all his clothes off quickly. Only until

the last sock. As he was completely naked, he tried to take off this last sock while still standing up. His massive body shape in combination with the stress of the moment, led to a disastrous result.

He tripped over himself and landed with his back down on the wooden floor with a massive bang.

"Everything ok Nicole??" the madam was heard shouting from outside with her gruff voice.

"Yes, yes, no problem." Nicole shouted back.

"Are you ok my love?" she asked Babis who had managed to get back up like a metallic spring. He was completely naked now, with his pyramid tits looking straight into Nicole's eyes.

"Yes! I'm ok! No problem!" he replied.

"What the hell?

How did I fall?

She must think I'm an idiot now..." he thought, while his back was already hurting from the free fall.

"Wow!" she exclaimed and continued: "What a nice body you have!" She then pushed him gently on the bed. As he laid down on his back, she grabbed his willy, which was still on a sleep mode, and started massaging it.

"Relax now my love... Nicole will make you hard!" she promised in her deepest, sexiest voice possible.

Babis, with his eyes closed, managed to relax slightly and enjoy the professional massage, which finally led to an acceptable erection after almost two and a half minutes of effort.

"That's it my sexy boy! Now you make sweet love to Nicole my baby!" she said and jumped on top of him after she placed the necessary condom.

"I love it my boy! It's so big!" she encouraged Babis, while moving back and forth on top of him. "That's it sexy boy, that's it! Don't stop my stallion!"

"Does she seriously feel anything?

Is she lying to me just because I paid her?

What is 'stallion'?

Why she called me 'stallion'?

Is it good to be 'stallion'?

And I can't stand the sound of her tits.

They sound like someone is clapping his hands for me.

Oh no!

Nooo...

Nooooo!

No! No! No! No! No! No!...

 Noooooo..." and that's when his inner monologue came to an end.

Nicole stopped moving with immediate effect and jumped off him.

"What's wrong with you? Eh boy? Are you taking the piss now or what?" she asked him fairly pissed off. "This has never happened to me before! I can't believe you! Are you for real you little prick?" she continued with her rant.

"I'm sorry, I'm sorry, I don't know why this happened..." replied Babis looking at his dead as a doornail penis. It was now looking down towards the bed mattress, totally sad and wrinkled, having lost all the glory it had gained almost a minute ago.

"You need to respect women like me. You can't come here and treat me like this. You can't come here after you had sex with your girlfriend or had a wank. Shame on you!" Nicole snapped at him.

She got up and put her fish-net-kimono back on. Before she left the room, she turned towards Babis and said extremely annoyed: "Just so you know little boy, *i gria kota ehi to zumi!*" *(η γριά κότα έχει το ζουμί.) [literal translation: the old hen has the juice. This phrase is used in Greece to state that old women are better lovers and make better sex than the younger ones.]* And then, she stormed out of the room.

Babis jumped out of the bed, put his clothes back on as fast as possible and rushed out of the room like hell. He ran through the waiting room where the madam was sitting in the same armchair, reading her newspaper and still smoking. She only lifted her head to watch his rapid escape out of the brothel. When he was finally out of there, she took a deep cigarette puff and continued reading her newspaper.

"This was a big mistake... A big stupid mistake... I shouldn't have listened to malaka Tasos... I shouldn't..." Babis stated to Lakis who was waiting outside, under the shadow of a tree.

"What happened? asked Lakis.

"I'll tell you everything later because I can see him coming. Don't say a word to him! Please don't!" Babis stared into Lakis's eyes, willing him to keep his mouth shut.

"Wow!! Wow!! Wow!! shouted Tasos making a wolf howling and then continued: "That was awesome!! I wanna go back in!!"

"Me too!" said Babis as truthfully as he possibly could.

"I know! Wasn't it craaaazy?" responded Tasos in full excitement. He then suggested to the other two: "Let's shoot from here! We'll discuss everything on our way back! And I'm so sorry for what you missed Lakis..."

During the return journey, Babis made up a believable story which included everything Tasos wanted to hear about his 'glorious, unbelievable, once in a lifetime sex'.

The next day, Babis met with Lakis and explained everything in detail. This awful experience brought them closer than ever and agreed that they would never tell Tasos the entire truth. And they never ever again followed him to his regular visits to the brothels after that 'victorious' day.

8:13pm, Thursday 13th May 2010

When Babis was convinced that Tasos wouldn't shoot off into outer space like a rocket, he released his shoulders.

"How the bloody hell did this happen? Explain quickly malaka!" asked Babis.

Tasos was expected to describe what had just happened between him and Barbara in the simplest and quickest way possible. "Well, Barbara.... What a woman! Her long red hair... Her body like a twenty-year-old lingerie model... Her angel face... How many men must have been beating their meat just with the thought of her for years and years... And you must have done the same because I definitely have soooo many times!"

Babis cut him off in the middle of his response. "Yes, ok malaka. Whatever you say. But how could you..."

"Let me finish!" Tasos stopped him abruptly. "You know we're friends on social media and until recently we just liked each other's posts and two months ago, you remember I had the big tattoo starting from my left shoulder down to my elbow? And that I posted some photos of me showing the tattoo with no top on? Didn't I look completely ripped in those photos?" Tasos expected a serious answer from Babis at that point.

"What a malaka is this! Tell me quickly what happened you bastard!" Babis answered furiously to Tasos' narcissistic question, even if he was well used to this kind of questions from him. Tasos' self-confidence about his body shape was still low, even though he was completely ripped. The reality was that after all the years of intense body building, his body was eligible for the front cover of a men's magazine.

"Ok, ok, ok." Tasos realised that he was going out of topic and returned to the main body of his short (probably not) explanation.

"After that post, Barbara did something she hadn't done before and apart from a 'Like' on my post, she went on and sent me a private message saying to me things like *'well done for your hard work'*, *'the time you have been spending at the gym has absolutely paid off'* and *'this tattoo design looks wonders on you'* and shit like this and I was very surprised, but also super confused with this and that's why I never said anything to you then and after that message, we have been messaging each other almost every day with boring messages about daily shit and then we shared some photos with our gym outfits and how good we both look in them." at this point Tasos paused to take a much needed deep breath again.

This gave Babis the opportunity to say: "Are you serious? You sent these photos to Lupo's wife you idiot?"

After Tasos refilled his lungs to the maximum with a mixture of oxygen and the citrus toilet spray air freshener which just sprayed the half-hourly scheduled dose inside the small toilet space they were in, he continued his short (definitely not) explanation, without even replying to Babis' question. "You know today it's their wedding anniversary and they have invited me and my parents to have dinner with them and Lakis, here at 8:30pm, which is in fifteen minutes and Lakis thought it would be a brilliant idea to go out and get pissed with the other lads at Diablo Bar before we meet here because he wanted to celebrate for his parents' anniversary and I had five or six mojitos, I think, and many tequila shots, but we had to end it because it was almost 7pm. I said to Lakis that I wanted to walk back home to get some fresh air to cool my head down from the booze and he left me alone because he would drive the other lads back home with his car. If I only knew what would follow because when I was walking by the park I met Barbara, who was out to buy cigarettes and we started talking and I was very excited to see her, probably overexcited because of the booze and she asked me to walk with her back home through the park and *'around the little lake to enjoy the scenery'* she said and it was so nice there and we were chatting and laughing about things that I don't remember now, until we reached the kiosk at the end of the lake and then she grabbed my right hand and said with a low sexy voice *'Come with me babe'...*" at this point he paused for one more time to take another deep breath.

This gave Babis the opportunity to say: "What the f..."

After Tasos managed to refill his lungs to their maximum capacity with a mixture of oxygen and the citrus toilet spray air freshener, he continued his long explanation without giving Babis the chance to say anything further than *'What the f...'*: "And she took me to the bench behind the kiosk and we sat down next to each other and then her face came close to mine and she closed her eyes and her lips touched mine! Wow! I didn't have time to think what was happening and after this it was only instinct and I was like a proper animal and I didn't think of anything and she jumped on me and we ended up having sex like there's no tomorrow and at the end she gave me the best blowjob I ever had and she told me I have the best abs she had ever seen and I got even harder after she said this and because I was sitting on that stupid bench, I came all over my pants... I can't believe it... Everyone will know now! Everyone will find out! Lupo will murder me! No! My parents will kill me! Oh shit... Lakis will definitely kill me too! Today's my last day on Earth! What have I done???" Tasos was seconds away from fainting. The colour on his face went from scarlet red to a porcelain tone in milliseconds, with the sweat running down like he was inside a sauna. He only wished for one thing: *'na anixi i yi na ton katapii'. (να ανοίξει η γη να τον καταπιεί) [literal translation: the earth should open and swallow him. This phrase is used when somebody has done something completely shameful and would rather disappear so nobody can see them again.]*

Babis, after listening very carefully, realised that his semi-drunk-sex-machine best friend was not many steps away from an absolute catastrophe. Nikolas, a.k.a. 'Lupo', and Barbara had been together for almost thirty years. Nikolas, a.k.a. 'Lupo', was also one of the most notorious and fearful 'businessmen' in Athens, the Greek capital.

You're with me now Barbara

"There's nothing I'd like to do here. I hate this village and you know this mum. I want to move to Athens! I want to go and study there!" said Barbara to her mother very intensely.

"Are you out of your mind? Your father will go mad. You know him very well. He'll never accept this. He's made all these plans for you here in the village. Do you forget that he bought all that land to make the business bigger? Do you forget he wants to put you in charge? Do you forget that he's finishing the extra floor in our house for you to live when you get married and have kids? How can you forget all these things Barbara?" asked her mother, Froso.

"Because I haven't forgotten any of these things, that's why I want to leave this miserable village. He's made plans for me without me. I never wanted to become a big farmer and I never ever wanted to stay here for the rest of my life like you and him. How many times have I repeated all these to you? But you always said to me: *'You're going through a phase'* and *'You'll think straight soon'* and *'Your future is here next to your family'* and *'Your dad has made great plans for you'*… You know what mummy? Screw all these!" exclaimed Barbara.

"Language!! shouted Froso back at her.

"Yes, yes, language! That's your problem! Language…" complained Barbara and then she continued: "You know what? Now it's the time to tell you my plan mum! Both of you agree that the right thing for me is to go and study in Athens or I just pack my things one night and go to live there without even saying goodbye to any of you! You choose." Barbara's words were like bullets, fired with precision and intent.

Froso realised that her daughter was pretty serious, probably more serious than ever before. Deep inside, she was filled with joy and satisfaction that Barbara wanted to chase her dreams and desires. Something she never did and was regretting almost every day, since she was a teenager at Barbara's age. She always wanted to support her, but she knew that it would be a massive struggle to persuade her father to do the same.

"Even if I agreed, how can I change your dad's head? You know him…" she responded sounding relatively troubled.

"Because I know him, I have the solution for you. You'll tell him that I need to study in Athens so I become more skilled to run his 'great business'. You'll also tell him that I'll return to the village after I complete my studies no matter what. And because I know you're very good at it, you'll make him think that he came up with this 'brilliant plan' all by himself. No matter what, I'm not staying here!" stated Barbara in the most decisive way she had ever used in the seventeen years she was alive. There was no turning back for her…

It was very common in the traditional patriarchal Greek families for the father to believe that he's the one who's having the upper hand and making all the important calls. But usually, the actual captain of the ship was the wife. By using her feminine influencing skills in the right way, she could manipulate her husband to her own secret agenda without him realising it. What truly happened was that she made the 'man of the house', the 'lion of the jungle', the 'king of the castle' believe that everything was originally his own idea and that he was so smart for coming up with such an incredible solution. But it was all hers, from A to Z.

Androklis, Barbara's father, was usually an absolute pain in the ass. Nine out of ten times, he was as stubborn as a donkey when it refuses to move backwards or forward. It was very difficult, almost impossible to change his mind at any given time. But her mother was the only one who could lead him to the direction she thought was the best each time.

Androklis was a typical old-fashioned, conservative and deeply religious Greek man born in the 1930's. He was always underestimating his wife's power in shaping the future of their family and that's the reason he was usually played by her. One of his biggest complexes was to show to all the people in the little village they lived and had spent all his life, that he's the leader of the family and every decision was made by him.

It took Froso almost three months to achieve the target and finally make him announce his important decision *'for the good of the business'* to his daughter. The announcement came at the right timing for Barbara to escape from the future her father had planned for her without her and be able to make all the necessary arrangements for her relocation to Athens. She was going to live with her auntie Sofia, Androklis' younger sister.

Sofia had been a widow for the last seven years and her heart was as empty as her house. Having Barbara living with her, would bring light in her life and fill the void inside her. She had no kids and always considered Barbara like her own daughter. Barbara, for her part, was eager to move in with her aunt. She had always gotten along better with Sofia than her own parents. She was a very open-minded woman and sincerely understanding towards Barbara, since she was a little girl. Sofia was always against her brother's plans for Barbara. She could tell from the early days that this girl was a very special one and would never fit in the village life her father had predefined for her.

But living in Athens in the 1970s wasn't easy as well. The city was polluted, overcrowded and economically unstable. The smog was so thick that it could be seen from miles away and it often caused respiratory problems to the Athenians. The population had more than doubled in the last two decades, due to a brutal economic migration from the countryside. This led to overcrowding, traffic congestion and a shortage of housing. Greece was also in a period of economic recession, which led to unemployment and financial hardship for a big number of people.

To make matters worse, the Greek Junta, a right-wing military dictatorship, ruled Greece from 1967 to 1974. The Junta was corrupt and repressive to an unprecedented degree. It cracked down on dissent as numerous people were imprisoned or exiled for their political beliefs. Makronisos, a small and deserted island close to Athens, was the main place were the Junta officials imprisoned and tortured thousands of their dissidents. Whoever didn't have the Certificate of Social Attitudes verifying that they weren't communists or communist sympathisers, could end up with serious trouble with grave consequences. This included their family members and usually people from their close social circle. At the same time, the Junta contributed to the economic problems in the wider city of Athens, as it set barriers to financial growth and investment to a high extent.

It was the start of August in 1970 when Barbara decided to move to her auntie's flat. A well-established Greek tradition in August, especially in the middle of the month, was that Athens went almost empty. This was due to two main reasons:

1st. August was the hottest month of the year in Athens, with scorching temperatures that can reach 40°C (104°F).

2nd. The Dormition of the Theotokos. This was a major feast day in the Orthodox Church and it was celebrated on August 15th each year. On this day, the Orthodox Christians gathered in churches to commemorate the death of the Virgin Mary and to pray for her intercession. The feast day was also a time for family gatherings and feasting.

Therefore, the city looked like it's under a strict quarantine due to a dangerous virus. Many businesses were closed for the entire month and the Athenians left the city for their summer break like the mice escape the ship before it sinks. The only difference with the mice was that the Athenians returned at the end of August and the city descended into chaos again.

Her new neighbourhood, despite being in the suburbs of a metropolis like Athens, had many similarities with the village she grew up. There was a square in the town centre which was the main meeting place for the locals and where all the kids and teenagers, between five and eighteen years old, were playing and hanging around. Around the square, there were several local shops like a bakery, butcher, green grocer, mini-market, clothing and shoe stores. In the centre of the square, there was the big orthodox church of Saint Nikolas.

In this town, everyone was connected with each other, one way or another. If they didn't know someone directly, they knew someone else who did. And with this kind of connectivity came a lot of gossip. Unstoppable and relentless gossip. Everyone knew everyone else's business and it was impossible to keep anything as a secret within this micro-environment.

"I think I'm ok for clothes for now. It's so hot I barely need to wear any! But I do need to buy new ones for the winter. I definitely need to visit the big stores in the city centre soon. At least the ones that are open. I have a big list to go through. Auntie, will you come with me? You know I love your opinion, especially when it comes to clothes!" said Barbara during the lunch she was having with her auntie Sofia.

"Of course, my dear! It's always my pleasure to stroll downtown from shop to shop. And now with you being here, it'll be fantastic! This period is perfect. It's very quiet and there're loads of good discounts as well. The only thing is that we must go either early in the morning or late in the afternoon because of the heat. Walking in this concrete jungle of a city centre, it'll feel like being roasted in a burning oven in hell, believe me!" replied Sofia very excited with the idea of going shopping with her niece.

"That's perfect auntie! I love you so much! I don't know how to thank you for what you've done for me! I still can't believe I escaped from that prison. And if it wasn't for you, I'd be soon smelling like a goat and probably think like one too!" said Barbara and hugged Sofia tightly, giving her a kiss in her left cheek.

"The pleasure's all mine my dear! I never liked that village anyway. Almost all people there are cavemen." replied Sofia and they both giggled to the sound of the word 'cavemen' as it was such a precise description of the natives of their village.

"Ah, there's another thing as well. Today around 7pm, my good friend Georgia and her nephew Nikolas will pay us a visit. I've told her about you coming to live with me and we both thought that it would be really good for you to be introduced to Nikolas. I know he's a bit naughty, but he has a good heart. I know him since he was a little boy. He's been through a lot, but he's a strong lad. Everyone knows him in our town and he's very well connected with people who run the show here. I believe he'll help you understand more about the locals and our place. He'll also look after you if needed. But I'm sure you won't need that because you are a tough woman. Are you ok to meet with them today?" asked Sofia.

"Is he good-looking?" asked Barbara without hesitation as she thought of her auntie more like a best friend rather than her father's sister.

Sofia replied: "You can judge for yourself dear! *Peri orekseos, kolokithopita!*" (*περί ορέξεως, κολοκυθόπιτα*) [*literal translation: regarding appetite, courgette-pie. This Greek proverb means that when it comes to taste, there are no rules and standards, and everyone can like whatever they want.*]

This discussion took place around 10am in the morning and they both spent the remaining time until the visit, tidying up the house and preparing some bits and bobs to treat their guests later.

With this and that, the time was already 6:30pm. Barbara went to have a quick shower and get ready. She was such a beautiful creature that she didn't have to do a lot to look pretty. She had long red hair, very bright skin, blue eyes and a baby face. With the shape of her body and height, 5ft 9' tall, she could easily become a model.

But Barbara's most beautiful element was her unique personality. She was very cool, giving the idea that she's a very innocent girl. She was usually quiet and enjoyed observing others without interacting much. She kept this approach with most people, but with those who   felt comfortable with, she would reveal her real self, the firecracker she was inside. A funny, bold, sarcastic woman who loved to shock people with her jokes and swearing.

The grandfather clock in Sofia's living room tolled seven times, echoing through the house like the sound of distant bells. It was seven o'clock and everything was in place. Nuts in glass nut holders and four different flavours of homemade cookies in porcelain deep dishes were neatly arranged on the main table in the living room. The air inside smelled of a combination of jasmine, from the air freshener Sofia had just sprayed everywhere, and orange cake, which was ready in the kitchen oven.

When the bell rang, Sofia ran to open the door to her guests.

"Welcome! Welcome! Come inside! Don't stand there!" cheered Sofia full of excitement and hugged Georgia. The two women exchanged two air kisses, a warm Greek greeting that shows affection and respect. Then Sofia did the same with Nikolas.

"Let's go to the living room. It's still roasting outside to sit at the balcony. I have the fan on, it's nice and a bit cooler in there." suggested Sofia and led them to the living room where Barbara was waiting for them.

"Oh, my darling Barbara! It's so nice to meet you at last! Sofia has told me so many great things about you! Oh God! Aren't you gorgeous or what?? Welcome to our neighbourhood!" cheered Georgia when she saw Barbara standing next to the big dining table. Georgia then hugged and kissed her in both cheeks as she was supposed to.

When Nikolas entered the living room and looked at Barbara, he stopped moving. His eyes and mouth opened slightly, and his heartbeat must have exceeded one hundred and fifty beats per minute.

He wasn't expecting this at all...

Nikolas was twenty years old, with a heavy built and gym body, 6ft tall, with short brown hair. He wasn't a classic beauty, but he was a character who could light up a room. Due to his connections and history, the locals respected him despite his very young age, as his involvement with the organised crime was a common secret. When meeting people, he was always confident, very outspoken and whenever needed, cocky. But not today.

"Oh.

My.

God.

What's going on here?

What's this creature?

I can't believe how pretty she is...

Is she real?

What will she think about me?

I wish she doesn't think I'm as ugly as a beast.

What am I saying to her now?

I need to find something clever to say to her.

Screw it.

I'll say nothing for now.

Maybe a bit later." he thought standing there, frozen, for three full seconds, unable to tear his eyes away from her.

Barbara's beauty struck him like a thunderbolt. She was so ethereal, looking like the goddess Aphrodite, who had descended straight from Mount Olympus. Finally, after what felt like an eternity, he managed to snap out of it and, at least, shake her hand.

When he heard her sweet voice for the first time, saying to him with a beautiful smile: *"Hi Nikolas! I'm so happy to meet you!"* he felt like a siren was calling him and was instantly hooked.

He already had a crush on her.

"I don't believe it!

She smiled at me!

And she's happy to meet me!

I love it!

Love it!

Love it!

Love it!

Malaka Nikolas.

Don't say anything stupid and ruin it now for God's sake.

It goes well so far!

So shut the hell up and stay quiet for now.

Just give her your telephone number before you leave.

Then ask her to go out for a coffee.

That's all.

Don't say anything more now.

If you scare her away, I'll kill you bastard!" he thought and sat quietly on a chair next to the main dining table.

Nikolas followed his plan to the letter. He was a silent observer, not saying a word and letting the three women do all the talking. He knew that if he wanted to learn more about Barbara, he needed to be patient and let her reveal herself in a more appropriate time, without their aunties around.

Throughout the duration of the visit, he was pretending to listen to the aunties' discussions with increased interest, but his eyes were glued to Barbara. He couldn't help but watch her every move, mesmerized by her beauty. Anyway, the two aunties, being authentic Greeks, were so loud and animated that Nikolas's daydreaming went completely unnoticed.

The visit didn't last for long and when it came to an end, Nikolas put into motion the final part of his masterful plan. "This is my home telephone number Barbara. You can call me anytime. If I'm not there, leave a message for me and I'll get back to you as soon as possible. We can go grab a coffee or a bite in the following days. Whenever you're free and in the mood, of course, to see my not-so-petty face again..." suggested Nikolas just before they exited the door, when his aunt Georgia was busy talking to Sofia.

"Oh Nikolas! Please don't say that my dear! It was an absolute pleasure to meet you today! And don't be silly! I would love to meet you again one of the following days! I just need to sort out a few things and when ready, I'll call you to meet for a coffee. And without the aunties around. Deal?" responded Barbara and winked at him with a cheeky and sweet smile.

"Deal!" replied Nikolas excitedly and made an unexpected move to give her a friendly hug before they left. Barbara didn't hesitate at all and they found themselves awkwardly hugging each other for just a couple of seconds, in a friendly, but strangely intimate manner.

They both smiled at each other, said their goodbyes and that was it. He knew from this moment; she was the one for him.

Love at first sight had happened to Nikolas...

The day after, it was around 2:30pm when Barbara was walking back home from the mini-market in the town centre. The streets were a ghost town, abandoned to the blistering heat that poured down like molten lava from the burning Athenian sky.

To cope with this extremity, Barbara was dressed quite lightly, wearing hot shorts and only a belly top. Despite the intense heat, she had her long red hair loose. She never liked it in a ponytail because it reminded her of the village and her mother. She was like a cool breeze on this super-hot day.

When she turned a corner, two young men, around seventeen to eighteen years old, were walking towards her. One of them was short and chubby, and the other was tall and skinny. When they saw her, the short man started catcalling her and the tall one wolf-whistling at her.

Barbara wasn't used to such abuse. She grew up in a small village where everyone knew each other, and it would have been murder if someone did that to her.

After the first shock and instinctively thinking of turning around and walking away from them, she thought again.

"No.

No!

I'm not running away.

And I'm not a coward!

If I ran away, they won't stop.

They'll follow me.

And then it'll be worse.

I'll continue walking.

Anyway, what will they do to me?

It's just two boys.

And I'm in the middle of the town.

That's it.

Screw them both!

I'll continue walking and ignore them."

This was a bold decision for a seventeen-year-old girl in a new town, with no idea of who is who or what is what. A decision that would change her life forever...

"What road should I take to reach your heart babe?" shouted the short one.

"You are so hot that I get a nice tan when I look at you!" followed the tall one when they had almost reached Barbara, who didn't stop walking at any point.

The short man stood in front of her and cut her way and the tall one moved to her side. Now she was almost surrounded by them. She tried to change direction to cut through them, but the short one moved again, cutting her way for one more time, forcing her to stop.

"Apart from creating earthquakes when you walk around like this, what else are you doing in your life, love?" continued the short man without caring about the fact that they were both verbally abusing her.

"Can I ask you babe? Are your shorts from outer space? I'm just asking because your ass is from another planet!" said the tall one who was almost behind her, staring at her bum. The two boys burst out in laughter after this last comment.

Barbara felt shock and terror simultaneously. She shed a tear and regretted her decision not to turn around and run away from them. She realised that she was by no means prepared to deal with such raw abuse. She was now frozen by the fear of what they might do to her with nobody around to help. The street was completely empty and all the windows at the flats and houses around them were sealed, due to the extreme heat.

The short one approached her very closely. He then brought his face extremely close to hers and said: "Can I give you a little kiss to check if you are as sweet as you look baby?"

And that's when Barbara burst out crying.

The very loud noise of a big motorbike revving as it was approaching them, made the two men stop to look who was riding towards their direction.

It was Nikolas.

They could easily tell from the sound that it was him as his motorbike was known to the local youngsters. He also had no helmet on. By the way, almost nobody was wearing helmets when riding motorbikes in Athens in the 70's. And the 80's. And the 90's. And the 00's. And the 10's.

"What's going on here?" asked Nikolas angrily when he stopped with his motorbike next to them before he even got off of it.

The two men completely froze. They knew very well who was Nikolas. And from the tone of his voice, they realised they might be in big trouble.

Nikolas then looked at Barbara. When he saw her tears, he set off like a firework.

He jumped off the bike and grabbed both from their necks. He then stuck them brutally against the wall behind them. This gave Barbara enough space to move away from them. Nikolas was looking at them with the same intensity a tiger looks at its prey, just before the attack.

The sound of Nikolas' two palms landing on their cheeks, must have woken half of the Athenians who were peacefully taking their siesta in the houses nearby. It was clearly heard in the silence of this hot Greek afternoon as he slapped them both at the same time using both of his hands, demonstrating an exquisite technique of face slapping.

After the slaps were successfully completed, he grabbed them both from their necks again.

"Do you know her, you little bastards?" said Nikolas without raising his voice. And, for the second time now, he gave them both the same slap in synchrony.

"Ni.. Ni.. Nikolas... we... we are sorr..." tried to say the short man and they both received the third slap, before he even managed to complete his sentence.

"Shut up you fat malaka." said Nikolas using the same steady tone and grabbed their necks again. Only this time, he applied more pressure to their throats and they both coughed uncontrollably.

They both knew that if they fought back against Nikolas, they would be making a fatal mistake. They just had to swallow their pride and follow his orders, no matter how humiliating or dangerous it seemed.

"Listen now very carefully. Both of you. If you ever see this girl again, you will change direction and disappear. If she ever tells me that you even looked at her, I'll end you both." and that's when they both received the fourth and strongest slap of all so far.

"Do you understand me, you stupid sons of bitches?" asked Nikolas while he was still chocking them against the wall.

"Yes! We do! We do!" they both answered in symphony as if they had been rehearsing for this moment many times before.

"Now get the hell away from here. And I don't want to see you two pieces of shit around this neighbourhood again. Go!" said Nikolas and before he even finished his sentence, they had both started running away on full speed.

"Are you ok Barbara?" Nikolas asked her with a completely different tone of voice, in a calm and caring manner, and moved towards her.

Barbara couldn't help herself. She threw her arms around him and squeezed him tightly. She then buried her face in his shoulder and sobbed, with the whole of her body shaking with emotion. Nikolas hugged her too and allowed her to calm down before he even said anything.

"I'm so sorry about all this... I honestly am. And I'm also sorry you saw me acting like that. But you don't have to worry about them now. They'll never come near you again. Trust me on this."

Barbara looked into his eyes and said: "Thank you Nikolas!"

She then moved her head close to his. She closed her eyes and kissed him on his lips. When she finished with the kiss, they stared into each other's eyes, lost in the moment. They hugged and kissed again. And this time they didn't stop...

"You're with me now Barbara." said Nikolas when they finished kissing and offered her his hand.

Barbara took it.

They both got on his bike and left the scene. Only physically because their thought would return back there for years and years.

Back to the place where they kissed for the first time.

8:21pm, Thursday 13th May 2010

"I know what to do with your pants and stop worrying about Lupo and Barbara for now because we have a bigger problem." said Babis.

"Are you a malaka now? I just had sex with Lupo's wife on a bench at the park on their wedding anniversary! What problem can be bigger than this for God's sake?" asked Tasos frustrated and confused at the same time.

"My mum." Babis replied sharply.

Soula was usually spending her free time during the evenings, hanging around at the taverna. She refused to have any kind of involvement with the operations, especially helping in the kitchen with cooking or anything else. She didn't want to get her hands dirty under any circumstances. Especially after the death of her husband Ilias in 1999, her approach to life was one without a lot of responsibilities. What she highly enjoyed though, was meeting with her other widowed friends in the taverna, to have a laugh and gossip about anything without mercy. Soula was a nosy woman and gossip was her bread & butter. She also cared about what other people thought of her and her family to a sick degree. All her friends were pretty much the same.

The bar area in the taverna was their favourite meeting spot. They loved it there as they could talk and laugh without directly disturbing any of the customers in the customer dining area.

But most of all, it was the best spot for them to complete their traffic control checks about who was going in and out of the taverna. When they had gathered all the relevant customer traffic data, they would proceed in deeper analysis of it. The key points of their detailed analysis were based on the following questions:

Who came with who at the taverna?

Why did they arrive together?

Why did they arrive separately?

Why did they come with them and not with the others?

What clothes did they wear?

How did their hair look like?

What did they order?

Did they look like they were on a date?

Did it look like they were cheating on their wife / husband?

Why were they arguing?

Did they seem like they were drunk?

Were they on drugs?

Did they look like they were trying to impress someone?

How much did they spend?

Were they trying to hide something?

How much could they be earning from their jobs?

Did they look like they were high-maintenance?

Are they doing any dirty jobs on the side?

and the list went on and on...

Babis was fully aware of Soula's love for gossip and how nosy she could be. Therefore, the less she knew about Tasos and Barbara, the better. The best-case scenario would be if she was kept completely in the dark. But that seemed to be quite a stretch.

"I still don't get it mate. She's not even here at the bar like every night. What's the problem with her?" asked Tasos.

"She's sitting at a table with her friends because one of them has her birthday today. I bet my ass they all watched you from the second you came in here like a malaka. So now, they must have one million questions and I know she's waiting at the bar outside because I saw her coming this way when we came into the toilets. And if I open this door now and get out of here, I'm in big trouble because she won't stop asking me what happened. I'm bloody stuck now... I don't know what to do... You had sex with Lupo's wife! I can't believe it you idiot! Stupid malaka!" Babis was so anxious that even his stallion mate was starting to look calm by comparison.

"Come on! You need to help me! Lupo will kill me when he finds out! Do you think I have enough time to run home, pack a bag and disappear?" Tasos asked with his voice trembling with fear, but his eyes determined.

Babis paused. He made a serious attempt to put his brain function in the right order to use the best of his decision-making mechanism.

He was facing:

A. An extremely busy taverna without enough staff and not being able to help.
B. Being stuck in the toilet with a semi-drunk Tasos who had royally screwed up in an irreversible way and couldn't be left unattended.
C. Soula, his nosy mother, who was sitting just outside and had recorded every move Tasos made from the main entrance to the toilets.

The most critical challenge of all was that Babis' CPU (Central Processing Unit) wasn't the fastest in the market. The risk of it overheating and finally collapsing, due to the severity and complexity of the tasks it had to complete, was rather likely to occur.

At least, he was aware of his weakness to deal with such complicated cases like this one. Consequently, to avoid a permanent damage in his main processor and avoid the risk of making a decision which could potentially have disastrous consequences, he needed specialist advice. In this case, the only one person who could possibly help him to get out of this pickle was his older brother, Vasilis.

"Listen carefully. This might be your lucky day and I'm not joking now because Vasilis told me he'll be here tonight and maybe he's already out there. So, listen carefully what I'll say to you now word for word. Get into one of the men's toilets and wait there until I'm back. It won't be long. I promise you. Take this dry cloth and use it to clean your pants from the cum. I'm using it to polish the wine glasses and it will do the job perfectly. Then, stand under the hand drier in there to dry your pants. Until you do all these, I'll be back. Do you understand?" asked Babis.

Where the hell is Babis?

Vasilis was born in 1980 and Babis followed eight years later. This age gap between them was relatively big and had a critical impact on their relationship all the way through.

During his early school years, Babis exhibited an extraordinary behaviour. Since he started primary school, he was waking up every single morning extremely worried. Most of the times, he would end up crying like a ten-month-old baby who had pooped his nappy and his bum was burning hot. This behaviour was based on his fear that his teacher had walked past their family home and had already arrived in school before he did, so he would end up being late for class.

The primary school was just five minutes walking distance away from their flat and Babis would just walk there by himself, despite his young age. During the 1990s everything seemed to be much more innocent in Greece, even in a big city like Athens. Parents would let their kids play outside their homes for hours completely unattended. They usually didn't have the slightest idea where they might be as they were wandering around the neighbourhood without specific geographical limitations. No mobiles were invented yet, so knowing where the kids were exactly located each time and being able to call them, were completely out of the question.

Eight out of ten times Babis would wake up around 7am in the morning and start his stressing-panicking-crying operation. This was relatively bearable as everyone was waking up at this same time during the school days anyway. Their usual approach was to calm him down by playing on repeat the exact same tape, which included the following soothing statements in this specific order:

Don't worry Babis.

The teacher hasn't passed our home yet.

You won't be late.

Stop crying.

Go wash your face and teeth.

And let's have some breakfast.

Ok?

It would normally take Babis a good five minutes to return to his normal state from the stressing-panicking-crying mode. While he was in it, he was acting like he was sleepwalking in a sense.

Soula was the first responder whenever this happened. She would always try to calm him down with a sweet voice and a hug. She was feeling sad for what her baby was going through and her maternal instinct didn't allow her to do otherwise.

His dad Ilias though, wasn't truly involved in any of the efforts to calm him down. He just couldn't be bothered. Consequently, he usually let Soula deal with it. He wasn't showing that he was annoyed by the whole situation, but there had been a couple of times when he couldn't control himself and had shouted angrily at little Babis.

The result was a big argument between him and Soula, where he received the following serious warning: if he behaved like that again, she would impose extreme measures on him, including no sex for six months minimum. This proved to be a very effective way of negotiation as he took very seriously the risk of turning to a six-month-masturbator, if he shouted again at little Babis during any of his episodes in the mornings.

So far, so good.

But they all had a bigger challenge to face with little Babis, who wasn't actually so little. Compared to the rest of the eight-year-old kids in his class, he looked like a little giant, weighing almost ten stone and being 5ft 5' tall. There have been several instances, when he would wake up a bit earlier than 7am and enter the stressing-panicking-crying mode.

A bit earlier means, he had woken up literally in the middle of the night, like 4am or even 3am. His personal waking up record time was at 1:30am on a Sunday night. That was an absolute killer for everyone in the family, especially just before a dark, miserable and wintery Monday morning.

Vasilis and Babis were sharing a bedroom in the flat where the family lived. This meant that Vasilis was usually the first one to be affected from all this. And he wasn't enjoying it in the slightest. He had lost his sleep several nights and most of the mornings, he was waking up anxious as well.

Deep inside him, he was feeling sorry for his little brother as he loved him and certainly cared for him. But at the same time, he was extremely annoyed by the whole thing. He had never expressed his anger towards Babis, but he was like the Vesuvius volcano in Pompeii, ready to erupt at any given time.

Vasilis was sixteen years old and had already begun his rebellion mainly towards his father Ilias. This included secretly drinking alcohol, smoking cigarettes and occasionally weed. He was also going out with his mates until late, like 2am or even 3am, usually on Saturday nights. Especially the last one, was completely against what his father Ilias allowed him to do and had resulted in epic arguments between them.

Vasilis didn't seem to take his father, who called him 'Ilias the Prick', seriously. He just continued to ignore him, believing that he would just give up and let him do whatever he liked at the end.

Their relationship had never been on good terms and the biggest fault laid with his father. Since Vasilis was a little boy, Ilias acted most of the time in a very competitive manner against him. This was highly unreasonable and demonstrated his low quality as a father figure. He never had a proper conversation with his son, like normal humans do, for more than five minutes without ending it with an argument and shouting.

When Vasilis was younger, he experienced verbal and

physical bullying from Ilias, as he was smacked several times for insignificant reasons. Ilias' explosive temper towards his son, led Vasilis to dislike him from a very young age. When Vasilis grew up and became a teenager, things got significantly worse between them. Vasilis didn't tolerate his father's abusive behaviour and responded in a similar and sometimes worse way. A couple of times, they squared off like two raging bulls, with their nostrils flaring and their muscles tensed, ready to charge and pummel each other into submission. Only Soula's screams and tears prevented them from unleashing their full fury and harming each other irreversibly.

It was around 2:30am on a hot Saturday night in June 1996, when Vasilis returned home after a night of clubbing with his mates, which involved heavy drinking.

Just before they split, they smoked the final spliff of the night and as a result, Vasilis *'ihe klasi mali'. (είχε κλάσει μαλλί) [literal translation: he had farted hair. This phrase is used when someone is super-stoned, high as a kite, off their head.]* That weed was a local produce from Kalamata, with a very strong psychedelic effect, which could last for hours.

When he arrived home, he had to make every effort not to wake up the rest of the family, especially his father. This way, he would avoid another preaching session from him, which would definitely end up in a massive quarrel in the middle of the night. It was also certain that the intense Kalamata-weed-effect he was experiencing would not help him to be in the required physical and mental state to cope with such a demanding task.

After he entered the flat as quietly as possible, he tiptoed until he reached his parents' bedroom. When he was outside of it, he heard his father snoring like a full-grown crocodile. It never made sense to him how his mother, Soula, could sleep, almost every night, next to this beasty, straight from the jungle sound. He always believed that only a junkie after a strong heroin fix could achieve that.

His father's crocodile snoring made him feel sorry for her, but it was good news for him. His late arrival would go unnoticed by *'Ilias the Crocodile Prick'*.

But Babis had different plans for Vasilis. After moving in stealth mode from the moment he entered the flat, Babis suddenly woke up when he finally entered their bedroom. He was just about to enter his usual stressing-panicking-crying mode and this would destroy all the hard work Vasilis had put in so far to go completely unnoticed.

"What time is it? What time is it?" Babis asked anxiously and jumped out of his bed in his hot-dog-pyjamas. He was absolutely obsessed with hot-dogs. He had all the possible types of hot-dog-pyjamas, covering any spring, summer, autumn and winter collections.

"Did my teacher pass from here?" was his usual second question from the script he followed during every episode.

"He just passed Babis! You'll nearly make it to the bell! Come on hurry up!" replied Vasilis. "Come here, let me help you with your bag!"

Babis, who was now weeping, moved towards Vasilis to help him with his bag so he could be on time for school on a hot Saturday night in June...

"Come on little fella! You're ready now. Just put on your flip flops and walk fast! The teacher will start the lesson any minute now! Hurry up!" Vasilis encouraged his desperate to be on time for school brother.

Babis was moving around like a zombie on cocaine, fast and sleepy at the same time. He was probably sleep-walking, but Vasilis didn't seem to give two shits about it, as the whole setting was unbelievably hilarious for him. And this was the right opportunity to pay Babis back for all the sleepless nights and full of anxiety mornings he had because of him.

"Follow me Babis. I will take you outside fast so you can be on time. But you must move fast! I repeat! Move fast and don't stop to think for a moment because you will be late for school if you do! Do you understand?" Vasilis wanted to confirm that everything would go as planned in his intoxicated head.

"I do! I do! Let's go! I'm late! The teacher... I'm late!" Babis replied desperately, with the tears running down his big, round, shinny, red cheeks.

They got out of their room and moved quickly, passing their parents' bedroom, until they reached the main door of their flat. They lived on the third floor, so Vasilis knew that if he let him walk down the stairs alone in his state, he would certainly injure himself seriously. He had to send him off to school following at least the basic Health & Safety rules by assisting him to the elevator and letting him go when they had safely reached the ground floor.

"Come on! Hurry up! You need to go very fast now, or you won't make it on time and the teacher will punish you!" said Vasilis, after they exited their flat and closed the door behind them. "Hold my hand tight now and focus. You can make it little fella! Believe in yourself!" Vasilis encouraged Babis as they entered the elevator.

Vasilis, still high as a kite, could hardly keep himself from laughing as he watched his brother in the elevator, on a mission to go to school at 2:40am on a Saturday night. Babis was so focused to reach the ground floor so he could rush to his school, that he didn't notice his big brother secretly laughing with him.

"We're almost there Babis, hold on! Be strong! You're gonna make it little fella!" Vasilis continued mocking him while they were descending to the ground floor.

"Here we are. Come on Babis! Go fast now and don't look back! Just go straight to school! Go Babis! Go!" This was the last time Vasilis spoke to his brother before he departed for the primary school.

Vasilis laughed hysterically after Babis had moved to a safe distance and couldn't hear him. The sight of his little brother in his hot-dog-pyjamas and flip flops with his school bag on, walking towards his school in the middle of the night, made his sides hurt from the hard laughter.

He was too high to understand how stupidly irresponsible and risky his idea was. He believed that Babis would realise that something wasn't right and then return safely back home. No other technical details of how exactly this would happen and all the possible dangers his little brother was facing were taken into consideration by him whatsoever.

When he stopped laughing hysterically and lost Babis from his sight, he decided to go back to their flat and crush on his bed. He couldn't stop laughing at any point all this time.

The laughter stopped though when he reached the door of their flat.

He just realised that he had royally messed up. When they left the flat with Babis, he closed the door behind them and never took his keys with him.

His heart skipped a beat, his stomach dropped, his palms were sweating and felt like he was going to puke.

"What the fuck? How the fuck? What am I going to do now?" he spoke to himself as he was left locked outside. "Shit! Shit! Shit! How can I be so stupid! Everyone will wake up now! I can't believe how stupid I am for God's sake..."

As he was still stoned, he could have stayed there asking rhetorical questions to himself until Sunday lunch was ready to be served. But having no other choice, he did the most extreme thing he could possibly do.

He pressed the button from hell and rang the doorbell.

The sound of it felt so painful, like he was being stubbed repeatedly in the heart. He had never realised until then, how loud and lengthy was the sound of their bell. It felt like it was never going to stop ringing, a never-ending symphony. But that was probably the weed effect.

After almost thirty seconds, the door finally opened.

When 'Ilias the Awakened in the Middle of the Night Prick' opened the door and saw Vasilis standing in front him, he went ballistic.

"What time is this you little punk? Don't you have any respect at all for anyone in this house? And why the hell don't you use your own keys? Are you doing this on purpose to piss me off?" his father was so angry, he barely kept himself from slapping him in his face.

Vasilis didn't reply to him. He kept his red eyes down, looking straight at the floor, and walked past him, moving fast towards his bedroom.

"Where the bloody hell you go? Come here! Answer to me! Now! Don't ignore me malaka!" he continued shouting while he followed Vasilis to his bedroom.

When 'Ilias the Angry Prick' reached the kids' bedroom door, he realised that Babis wasn't sleeping in his bed.

"Where's Babis???" he asked Vasilis and before he received an answer, he ran to the toilet to check.

No Babis there too.

"Where the hell is Babis?" he screamed at Vasilis.

"He went to school." Vasilis replied.

"What???" 'Ilias the Very Angry Prick' shouted back like he didn't hear what he was just been told.

"He went to school." Vasilis repeated.

"What do you mean 'He went to school'? Are you completely drunk again? Speak to me now or I will punch you in the face, I swear! Where the hell is Babis?" 'Ilias the Furious Prick' shouted and moved aggressively towards Vasilis.

"He's on his way to school. I'm dead serious. If you leave now, you'll be able to catch up with him. He shouldn't be far away from here." Vasilis replied and laughed hysterically. The last image of Babis going to school in the middle of the night in his hot-dog-pyjamas, wearing his flip flops and school bag on his back, reappeared in his head.

"Are you joking now? I can't believe it! Did you send him to school so you can have a laugh malaka?" 'Ilias the Fuming

Prick' shouted again.

Vasilis tried to stop laughing, but he just couldn't as his father image made things worse for him. What he could see live in front of him was *'Ilias the Super-Fuming Prick'*, shouting at him in the middle of the night, wearing only a white underwear with a white pack vest on the top. This was emphasising his fat belly, which looked like he was due for a baby any minute. He was also wearing his plastic Greek army flip flops in brown colour, which were so worn out, he must have inherited them from his grandfather, who wore them when he fought in the First World War.

The crazy look of Ilias' sparse hair on his bald scalp was the cherry on the top of the cake. His hairstyle was entirely abstract, since he woke up so suddenly in the middle of the night. In Vasilis' stoned head, he looked like he was just blown in the face by a big cannon from the circus.

"You're in big trouble now! You really are! I'll deal with you in a bit! Wait until I'm back and you'll see..." his father threatened him and stormed out of the flat.

He didn't have the time to search for any clothes to put on. His little Babis was wondering alone in the middle of the night with his schoolbag on and this could have a nasty outcome for him. As a result, he left their flat with his crazy hair and sleeping gear on.

After *'Ilias the Exploring Prick'* departed for the sacred mission with a code name *'Searching for Little Babis In His Hot-Dog-Pyjamas & Flip Flops'*, Vasilis went quickly outside to the balcony, so he didn't miss any scene from the show. His mother Soula turned up and stood next to him.

"Oh, Virgin Mary! What's all this Vasilis? Jesus Christ! What's wrong with you? Oh God! Have you realised what you have done?" she asked him while she was repeatedly making the sign of the cross on her body, in the name of the Father, the Son and the Holy Spirit.

Vasilis looked at Soula and fell to his knees in laughter. He couldn't take her seriously, not with her hair sticking out in all directions and her sleeping gown hanging off her like a sack. She looked like a possessed nun to him and he couldn't help but find her hilarious too. Especially when she started calling on God, Jesus Christ and the Virgin Mary, and making the sign of the cross on her body. She seemed to him like she was speaking in tongues.

"Oh my God! Are you drunk? You're only sixteen... What are you thinking? From the time you stopped going to the church you have taken a very wrong path. Oh Jesus, please save my son! He's a good boy! He's just confused... I honestly don't know what to say to you Vasilis... What you did to Babis is so wrong! I hope he comes back home safe. Shame on you! I am very disappointed! And this time, I can't help you with your father when he's back. Be prepared for the worst..." said Soula and went back inside the flat.

Vasilis was still laughing even after she left. He absolutely didn't care about any of the points she made. He was highly confident that nothing bad would happen to his little brother. He was also determined to make the most out of this once-in-a-lifetime opportunity to entertain himself to the max.

His actions were the most selfish and uncaring his family had ever seen by him, as he displayed a shocking lack of concern for his loved ones, especially his little brother. Inside his own head though, he had already justified everything he did and believed that he had legitimate reasons for this kind of behaviour.

Not many seconds after, his father turned up at the car park of their block of flats, running in his sleeping gear with the crazy hair, shouting in the middle of the night: "Baabiiiiss! Baabiiiiss!" He continued running until Vasilis couldn't see him anymore. But he could still hear him as he continued shouting "Baabiiiiss!" unstoppably.

The entire neighbourhood heard him as well. Vasilis could see lights in neighbouring flats turning on. People were gathering at the balconies, to see what was going on. Vasilis found the whole thing so amusing that he burst out laughing again.

After a couple of minutes, *'Ilias the Loud-In-The-Middle-Of-The-Night Prick'* stopped shouting.

"He must have found him!

Victory!

Now everything will come together!

I wish I had some popcorn!

Or one more spliff!" he thought and stayed at the balcony to watch all the details from their epic return. This is what the rest of the neighbours did as well. Some of them have even started conversations from different balconies, guessing what was going on.

All this time, Vasilis was hiding behind two tall plants in the balcony. He didn't want to be questioned by any of the curious, probably angry and certainly woken up in the middle of the night neighbours.

But he was certain about one thing; even though the neighbours were annoyed and angry at being woken up in the middle of the night by Ilias' loud shouting, they would all be compensated when they watched the duo returning from their epic night quest in their outrageous outfits.

One phrase was playing on repeat in his stoned head: *'tha yelasi ke to parthalo katsiki!'* (Θα γελάσει και το παρδαλό κατσίκι!) *[literal translation: Even the multi-coloured goat will laugh. This phrase is used when a situation is so grotesque and has reached such an impenetrable point of surrealism, that everyone will laugh no matter what.]*

And that's when his father in his underwear and pack vest on top, all in white, the worn-out plastic Greek army flip flops in brown colour and cannon-blown hairstyle, appeared at the car park of their block of flats with the treasure from the night quest: little Babis in his hot-dog-pyjamas, flip flops and schoolbag.

The neighbours were laughing at the image, some of them silently, some others more loudly. But they were all laughing, just as Vasilis had predicted. Then they all begun returning in their flats as the movie *'Searching for Little Babis In His Hot-Dog-Pyjamas & Flip Flops',* came to a happy ending.

Vasilis had to think very quickly now where he should wait in order to protect himself from his highly likely fuming father. He had to find a place where *'Ilias the Bloodthirsty Prick'* couldn't reach him as he was certain that his father would physically hurt him, if he fell into his hands.

The only place, which he had already tried in the past and offered him an acceptable level of security, was the round table in their living room. Vasilis had already been chased by his father around this table a few times, and finally, he managed not to be caught, after they had been running around like lunatics for several minutes.

And that's where he had positioned himself when Babis and Ilias entered the flat. Babis walked in first. He was weeping and went straight into his mother's hug, who was waiting to comfort him.

And then *'Ilias the Champion Prick'* followed. After all that midnight running and shouting, he looked like he was run over a truck. His hair was still a mess, his white underwear and white pack vest were rumpled, and he staggered as he walked in his almost destroyed now plastic Greek army flip flops. All in all, he looked like he was about to collapse.

He stood for a second and took a deep breath. Then he looked at Vasilis with a look that could easily assassinate him and said: "What you did today, I'll never forget. You are a disappointment to me. Don't speak to me again unless I speak to you." And left for his room.

Based on his father's reactions in less serious cases in the past, this wasn't exactly what Vasilis expected from him.

'Ilias the Silent & Sad Prick' didn't speak to Vasilis for two whole months after this incident. Any communication between them, took place only through Soula. Even after they spoke again, their relationship would never be the same again. It was kept at a very basic level for the following three

years, until June 1999, when Ilias suddenly died from a heavy heart attack.

Tasos, having no other choice, shook his head in agreement. He then looked straight into Babis' eyes and as the booze effect was clearing off him mainly in the form of sweat, begged with a shaky voice: "Help me brother. Please help me. I'm scared for my life…"

Babis left him there and exited the toilets. As he had predicted, Soula was already standing at the end of the bar. She was probably waiting to tear him apart with her questions. But she wasn't alone. Next to her, there was a man standing with his back turned towards him. He quickly realised that this man was his older brother, Vasilis.

His figure seemed to Babis like a Messiah, sent by one of the twelve Greek Gods who was on shift that night and had listened to the entire desperate conversation that took place in the toilets, some minutes ago. Simultaneously, he noticed that Sarantos and Angela had arrived to cover the busy shift and were already in the main customer area, taking orders.

Babis big heart sang with joy like a bird in the morning sky. This exact combination of events was exceeding what he had wished for. Now, he had the necessary time to speak to Vasilis about Tasos' grave foul. And once again, as countless times before, ask him for a solution to a complex scenario as his brain capacity wasn't adequate to deal with it.

At that specific point, his brain neurons produced a feeling of hope that everything would be alright in the end. This made his nipples go hard. So hard that they were about to burst through the fabric of his t-shirt, which was so tight that it clung to his body like a second skin made of cling film.

Babis was under the illusion that he had a gym body and chose to wear tight t-shirts while at work. This was based on the indisputable fact that he visited the gym once or twice a month. But the aftermath of each one of these scarce visits, led to the conclusion that he would be better off if he didn't go to the gym at the first place. After each gym session, his cravings were reaching unprecedented levels and he would eat the same quantity of food, a family of four would consume during their Christmas Dinner.

Babis walked on a fast mode towards Vasilis and Soula. His gigantic figure and peculiar way of walking when he was in a rush, made Vasilis' peripheral vision warn him that he was being attacked. He immediately raised his eyes to assess the level of danger from the thing that was moving aggressively towards his direction.

The moment they looked at each other, Babis' eyes sent a specific message to Vasilis' eyes:

"Stop whatever you're doing immediately and follow me. No questions. Now!"

This communication took place in such high speed that Soula, the taverna's high-quality, super-efficient and never-malfunctioning CCTV system, missed it all.

"What happened?

Where are they going?

Why didn't my Babis even speak to me?

And why Vasilis followed him without saying a word?

...

Oh my God!

Something bad has happened!

I'm sure!

This is why Tasos was looking for Babis.

And this is why they were locked in the toilets all this time.

And now my Babis, my baby, wants Vasilis' help!

My poor little baby...

What have you done now?

Did you get a woman pregnant?

But you don't want the baby?

And her father is looking for you?

He wants to hurt you because you dishonoured her?

Because she was a virgin?

Oh my God!

Jesus Christ, please help my son!

I'm begging you!

.....

I can't go back to my friends now.

No way!

I'm so embarrassed...

What if any customers watched everything?

And they know what my Babis had done to the poor girl?

Oh, the shame!

I'll wait here until they're back.

I'm not going anywhere..." thought Soula after she watched both of them disappear from her sight within seconds. Now, her heart was racing, her palms were sweating and all her senses were on high alert.

Who the hell are you grandpa?
Or should I say grandma?

It had been a week since Tasos, Lakis and Babis visited the brothels hoping to finally lose their virginity and prove their manliness to their world. Tasos was certain that he hit both of these two milestones. On the contrary, things didn't go as planned for Lakis, who vomited before he even entered the brothel, and Babis, who massively failed to maintain the required erection for such a demanding and elaborate task.

It was probably the most humiliating experience these two boys ever had. On their way back home that day, they swore never to discuss it ever again. They also agreed to keep Babis 'malfunction' hidden from Tasos as they were both certain that he would be an absolute pain in the ass and push them mercilessly to go back to the brothels to 'make things right'.

But something had changed between them since that disastrous day. They were always close, but after that 'Black Saturday', as they called it, they seemed to be even closer. The following days, they spent hours after hours together, doing different things or doing nothing at all. It seemed as if they both had an increased need to be with each other, without planning or actively chasing it. It just happened naturally.

A week after their traumatic experience, they were sitting on a remote bench at the local park, watching from distance the world go by. People were leisurely wandering around the little lake enjoying the sunshine, while youngsters of all ages frolicked, with their laughter and shouts filling the air.

At some point Lakis turned to Babis and said: "I don't want to sound weird or anything, but I feel like I can tell you anything."

"Always. You're my best friend." Babis answered after he looked at him surprised.

"Well, the thing is... I've been thinking a lot about what

happened last Saturday. And I've come to a realisation..." said Lakis looking down at his hands, twisting his fingers nervously.

"What you mean?" asked Babis after he raised an eyebrow.

Lakis took a deep breath and said: "I think I might be... Ehmm ... I might be... gay."

There was a moment of stunned silence between them. Babis didn't know what to say or how to react. Despite all the signs, he had never considered the possibility that his best friend might be gay.

"Please don't be mad. I can't help how I feel." pleaded Lakis looking Babis into his eyes.

"No... No... I'm not mad Lakis." responded Babis shaking his head. "I'm just... I'm just surprised. But it's all the same. You're still my best friend."

"Thank you Babis! I was so scared to tell you this..." said Lakis letting out a sigh of relief.

Babis put his arm around Lakis' shoulders. "You shouldn't be afraid. You can tell me anything. I'm always here for you. No matter what."

They sat in silence, each lost in their own thoughts. It wasn't long until Babis spoke up. "I have something to tell you too..."

"What is it?" asked Lakis and looked at him curiously.

Babis took a deep breath. "I think... I'm gay too..."

"Really??" Lakis' eyes widened in surprise and happiness at the same time.

"Yeah." Babis nodded. "I mean... I never liked women. I mean sexually. And that day at the brothel... I don't know... Something wasn't right for me. Tasos was pushing us too much... This malaka! But when I'm with you, everything feels good. You never push me like that."

"I feel exactly the same! And I never felt this way before with anyone else apart from you!" said Lakis and gave him a sweet smile.

They remained silent, but their hearts could be heard pounding with fear and excitement. They both knew what this meant, but they were too scared to say it out loud.

Finally, Lakis spoke up. "Do you think... Do you think we could be... together?"

"Are you asking me to be your boyfriend?" Babis looked at Lakis with his heart racing.

"Yeah. I know it's sounds weird... But... I can't help how I feel!" Lakis nodded and his eyes were shining with hope.

"Come here you!" said Babis and put his arm around Lakis shoulders. Their heads moved closer... And closer... And closer....

And they kissed.

Then they paused as their lips parted for a breath, but only for a moment. They locked eyes and were lost in each other's gaze. They exchanged a sweet smile and resumed their passionate kiss.

And they kissed... And kissed... And kissed...

But they soon realised that they had to stop. Two boys kissing in a public location in Greece, in 2002, could end up in real trouble.

Even though homosexuality in ancient Greece was accepted and even celebrated, in that current time, it was a huge taboo in the 'modern' Greek society. Superficially, modern Greeks were putting a strong emphasis on traditional gender roles and family values. As a result, any individual who was 'unfortunate' to be member of the LGBTQ+ community, was usually excluded and victimised by their environment, either close or wider.

In Greece, until 1951, being a homosexual could not only stigmatise you, but also make you a criminal. Although it was decriminalised at the time the two boys were sitting on the bench kissing each other, discrimination and prejudice against the LGBTQ+ community persisted to a high extent, especially in smaller towns and communities. On average, Greece was still a deeply conservative society and one fact that showed this was that there was only a limited number of visible representations of LGBTQ+ individuals in the media and public life. This lack of visibility made it challenging for LGBTQ+ people to find acceptance and support in their communities, as most of them would keep it secret, sometimes for their entire lives.

Another significant point was the limited legal protection these people had. While discrimination based on sexual orientation was technically illegal, there were no actual protections against hate crimes and any kind of harassment against the members of the LGBTQ+ community.

Therefore, homophobia was spread like a disease in most Greek communities. People in the LGBTQ+ community often experienced unfair treatment in different aspects of life, like jobs, housing, healthcare, school and education. This could have been in the form of direct mistreatment, like mean words or even physical harm, or it could be less obvious, like being left out of groups or not getting good job chances. The media also often showed them in negative or stereotypical ways, making them feel even more left out.

The Greek Orthodox Church, probably the most influential and one of the most powerful institutions in Greek society, strongly promoted conservative and, most of the time, extreme views on sexuality and gender. This worsened the stigma against LGBTQ+ people, as many priests were openly hostile towards the LGBTQ+ community. They condemned publicly homosexuality as a sin, resulting in their sermons and statements fuelling a culture of hate and discrimination.

"Homosexuality is a curse, a deadly sin, it goes against psychological and biological normality." is an example of a statement made by an orthodox priest in one of the main public television stations.

However, it goes without saying that not all orthodox

priests in Greece held these extreme views. There were also progressive voices within the church which advocated for greater acceptance and inclusion of LGBTQ+ individuals.

The result of homophobia being so highly prevalent within the wider society, was the numerous homophobic attacks in the whole of Greece. These attacks have been documented by human rights organisations and media outlets, and ranged from verbal abuse to physical violence. In some cases, the attacks were carried out by groups belonging to neo-Nazi organizations, which were thriving in Greece that period.

The two boys were sitting on the bench holding hands and chatting, enjoying each other's company, when they noticed a group of young men approaching them from some distance. They were five in total, and their ages were between sixteen & eighteen years old.

As they moved closer, the group became rowdier and louder. The two boys thought that they seemed to be looking for trouble. Then one of them shouted: "Hey faggots! What do you think you're doing?"

"What the fuck! Look at the shirt-lifters holding hands!" another one yelled.

Lakis and Babis without a second thought, stood up and walked away from them as fast as they could.

"You filthy gays! Go get a room perverts!" someone of them shouted.

Babis and Lakis tried to ignore them and kept walking, but the abuse continued stronger.

"Look at these two queers! Disgusting!" one of them yelled again.

"What the hell's wrong with you sissy-boys? Can't you find a girl to hold her hand?" another one shouted.

Lakis and Babis froze from fear. They were unsure of what to do. They hadn't experienced any harassment like this before. Babis turned to Lakis, who was visibly shaken, and said: "Keep walking fast. We need to get away from them."

But the five men were persistent and wouldn't let Babis and Lakis go easily.

"Come on guys! Let's have some fun with these girls!" one of them said and threw a rock at Lakis, narrowly missing his head.

Babis was furious. He turned around and shouted: "For God's sake! What's wrong with you? We didn't do anything to you!"

"You guys are sick. You shouldn't be allowed to walk around in public like this. You're going to burn in hell for your sins." one of the five men stepped forward and sneered at Babis.

Suddenly, almost out of nowhere, a small sized man with long grey hair in a ponytail, walked beside Babis and Lakis and then stepped in front of them. "Is there a problem here?" he asked, looking at the group of the five men.

"Who the hell are you grandpa? Or should I say grandma?" replied one of them and continued: "Are you a faggot too?"

All five of them burst out laughing hysterically.

The man turned his head towards Babis and Lakis and whispered: "Just leave. I'm a police officer. I'll take care of this."

The two boys didn't have much of a choice. They turned tail and fled with their hearts pounding in their chests. They knew that this man was godsend and they weren't about to test his divine will.

When the five men saw the boys running away, they went ballistic.

"What the fuck you just did grandma? You're in deep shit now!" shouted one of them and they all made a move to attack him.

When the man saw them approaching him, he pulled his jacket on the side with his right hand. This way, he exposed a gun that was holstered around his waist.

All five of them froze.

"Fuck!!" said one of them.

"Shit!!" said another one.

"Run!!" shouted the third one.

In perfect synchronisation, they turned around and sprinted away from him, with their feet pounding the ground as they raced towards the bushes. They didn't dare look back, knowing that the man was right behind them. Seconds later, they had disappeared into the bushes, not to be seen again.

Luckily, this time, the stone didn't find its target.

8:28pm, Thursday 13th May 2010

Vasilis followed Babis silently, while they passed through the busy kitchen, until they reached the external area at the back of the taverna, where all the deliveries were arriving.

"Spit it out. What's going on?" he asked Babis, after they both checked that nobody was around them.

"Ok. Tasos was out with Lakis and some others and he got drunk and then, when he was walking back, he met Barbara eh... and then they walked together in the park and then they had sex at a bench half an hour ago and she gave him a blowjob and he came all over his pants and then he freaked out and came straight here to find me eh.... and then I took him to the toilets because mum was watching everything and I don't have a clue now what to say to her... and the big problem is today Lupo and Barbara have their anniversary and they have a table here for 8:30pm and this is in two minutes ehhh... and the other problem is they have invited Tasos and his parents and Lakis is coming too." said Babis in almost one breath and no full stops used.

When finished, he took a deep breath and moved as close as possible to Vasilis. He looked straight into his eyes and grabbed both of his hands. His huge frame was almost shaking with fear as he pleaded "What do we do now?"

Vasilis was considered to be a crisis-ninja by Babis, as he was convinced that his older brother could sneak into any situation and strike with deadly accuracy. But this time, Vasilis was the one caught with his pants down.

After Vasilis heard Babis' story, he was completely lost for words. His eyes remained wide open, performing maximum contraction and kept staring at Babis. He didn't even blink. This made Babis even more nervous than he was before. He was expecting a cool Vasilis with a wise answer out of his pocket, which would magically sort out the mess.

"Vasilis! Vasilis! Come on! What happened to you? Speak to me!" Babis yelled as he simultaneously shook him, having firmly seized both of his shoulders. This was his desperate attempt to reboot Vasilis as he looked as if he had paused all operations.

And it actually worked.

After the strong shake from Babis' giant-size hands, Vasilis was back on. "Oh. Fuck. There's no time even to be shocked by what you just said. You must listen to me carefully now and don't throw at me any of your usual bullshit questions. Ok?"

"What you mean?" asked Babis annoyed.

"You know what I mean." replied Vasilis.

"I don't." said Babis.

"You do." said Vasilis.

"No, I don't." insisted Babis angrily.

"Yes, you do." Vasilis said for one more time totally frustrated.

"No, I don't." Babis replied again.

"And that's exactly what I mean. Honestly, just shut it and listen to me." Vasilis ordered him, already exhausted before they even began their discussion.

He took a deep breath to recharge his brain and continued. "The first thing we need to decide is what we're going to say to Soula." He rarely referred to her as 'mum', 'mummy', 'mother' or any other mother-like expression.

"What we say to her after we go back, will affect the future of all the people involved directly and indirectly in this fatal mess. You must have realised already that there's an existential risk for the two main heroes of this story. Have you?" asked Vasilis very seriously expecting just a simple 'yes' or 'I do' for an answer.

"What this 'existential' means?" was what he got back from Babis as an answer instead.

"Oh God help me! This is how it will go now?" Vasilis took

a deep breath as his brother's illiteracy was the last thing he was willing to deal with at that specific moment in time.

"Let's go again. We need to decide if we tell her exactly what happened, or we make up a believable story to cover this up. Both options entail significant risks. We must think carefully so the harm to all the people involved is the minimum possible. And don't ask me what 'entail' means because I'm about to punch you in the face malaka!"

"I wasn't going to ask you about it. I know what entail means! It comes from the word 'end' and 'tail' and it means 'what will happen at the end' because the tail is always at the end. I know this word, I'm not as stupid as you think I am!" Babis answered full of confidence and pride for his premium knowledge.

Vasilis didn't have the time and mainly the energy to deal with this anymore. He just ignored him. He only looked at him in the eyes for two seconds and, without a word coming out of his mouth, thought: *"What the hell my brother... Seriously..."*

Consequently, he had to use the full capacity of his own brain to decide what's best to say to Soula. A decision which would also affect Lupo, as they had a very close friendship for years.

Vasilis had always looked up to Lupo since he was a little boy and after his father died, their bond grew even stronger. Lupo stepped in to support Vasilis and Soula whenever they needed urgent help. Lupo was always there for them, no matter what and Vasilis knew they could always count on him in any case of emergency.

On the other side, based on the stories about him throughout the years, Vasilis was well aware what Lupo was capable of in case he was disrespected.

He also knew why Nikolas was called 'Lupo'.

You're a wolf Nikolas, a real lupo

Nikolas was born in April of 1950 and the area he was brought up was one of the roughest in Athens at that time. His father died in a very young age in 1962 and Nikolas was left to survive in extremely poor conditions, with a mentally ill mother and his two younger brothers.

As he had to replace his father from the early age of twelve and care for his family, his choices were limited. He had to go out to the streets and kick ass for survival. He ended up getting involved with the local gang, which was connected to one of the strongest crime organisations in Greece.

"Are you ready?" asked Makis, the top dog in the local gang. He was a tall, muscular man with a shaved head. He had a scar on his right cheek and a cold, hard look in his eyes.

"I am." answered Nikolas, who was almost fourteen years old.

"Tell me again what you do. Step by step. And slowly." Makis wanted to ensure little Nikolas wouldn't screw up his first solo assignment.

"I have already told you three times since yesterday. You must take me for an idiot." replied Nikolas frustrated.

"First thing. I must be 100% sure you know what you're doing. You can't blow this up. Second thing. This attitude of yours. I don't like it. You have one more chance. Tell me again what you do. Step by step. And slowly." ordered Makis angrily staring into little Nikolas' eyes.

"Ok, ok." replied Nikolas.

He realised there and then one of the most important rules; no backtalking if he wanted to remain part of the gang.

"I'll take the bag, put it on my back, get out of here, take my bike from outside and use the back route you told me to get to the Saint John's woods without using the main road. If I see any people I know, I just say *"Hi, you alright?"* and go. If I meet any good friends, I should stop to speak to them for a couple of minutes, so they don't get suspicious and then tell them that I'm late to meet my uncle and leave. If I see any police, continue cycling like they're not there. And don't look at them. At all. When I reach the woods, I'll take the first path to the left and continue until I find the stone slide. There'll be two men there waiting for me. I'll give them my bag and they'll give me theirs. I mustn't start any conversation with them and not respond if they make any comments. I need to take the bag and come back here the same way. That's it."

"Good." said Makis and gave little Nikolas a tap on the back." This is the bag. Don't open it. Listen to me. Do not even think to open it. And take this pocketknife with you. Just in case."

"I have my switchblade with me. But I'll take this too." said little Nikolas and put the knife in his left back pocket.

"Ok. The meeting is in thirty minutes. If you ride your bike straight there, it'll take you around twenty minutes from here. You have another ten if you need to stop and speak to anyone. Go now." said Makis and nodded with his head, showing Nikolas the direction he should move.

And that's exactly what Nikolas did.

"Do you seriously believe he'll be ok with them, all by himself?" Billy asked Makis after Nikolas had disappeared. He had been working for Makis for years and was his most reliable man in the gang.

"It's his first solo job. I wanna see what he's made of. I have already sent three of our men at the meeting point. They are hiding and if he gets into trouble, they will jump in. There's something different with this boy. I believe he can do the job without any trouble." replied Makis.

"Do you trust him with a kilo of smack?" asked Billy as he wasn't quite convinced yet about little Nikolas.

"I do. He knows very well what happens to him and whatever's left from his family if he tries to screw me." said Makis and walked away.

Nikolas followed Makis' orders and rode his bike using the back streets. He was very lucky not to come across anyone he knew so far. This helped maintain his stress levels at a normal degree.

Only until he took one of the last turns.

He bumped on his aunty Poppy, his father's sister. She was returning home from the church as it was Sunday morning. Poppy always had minor mental health issues, but after her brother's death, she became significantly worse and was under medication. In several instances, the drugs made her lose her sense of direction and time.

And this was one of them. She was in a completely wrong location based on where the church and her home were on the map.

"Oh! Little Nikolas! Oh! How are you my dear?" she shouted with her squeaky voice, when she saw Nikolas approaching with his bike. She then moved towards him with very fast steps.

"Oh shit! I can't believe this now! Shit! Shit! Shit!" whispered Nikolas before she got closer and could actually hear him.

"Hi aunty." he said to her when she reached him. Now, he had to pretend that he's not in a hurry, not to raise any suspicions in case someone was watching.

"I haven't seen you for soooo long my sweet boy! You grow so fast! Look at you!" She stretched her right hand and pinched his left cheek. Her voice was still as loud as when she was thirty feet away. "Oh! Come here you little one!" she yelled and grabbed Nikolas with her two hands. She then hugged and kissed him in both of his cheeks.

"I love you so much my little Nikolas! You look more and more like your father and after he die..." and that's when she burst out crying on Nikolas' shoulder.

Out of nowhere, a police car with two cops inside, took a turn, drove towards their direction and stopped right next to them. What the cops could see was a middle-aged woman crying in a boy's shoulders, almost in the middle of the road. The co-driver cop, who had a big fat black moustache, lowered his window and asked: "Is everything ok here madam?"

Aunty Poppy hadn't realised that the cops had stopped right next to them until she heard the cop's deep I-just-drank-a-bottle-of-ouzo-in-the-taverna voice.

She responded with the same high levels of decibels in her voice, no change. "Oh, Mr Policeman! Everything is ok here! I just met my little nephew Nikolas after I went to the church. I love him so much! He looks like my brother who die..." and that's when she started crying again on Nikolas' shoulder.

After a few seconds of weeping, she stood up again and continued yelling: "He's a very good boy Mr Policeman! And a very good student! Look! He has his schoolbag to go to school today!"

This last comment raised alarm bells for the cops. No schools were open on Sunday...

Nikolas almost shat himself.

But he realised quickly that he had to keep his cool. The cop with the big fat black moustache and the I-just-ate-a-bad-tzatziki voice, was now scanning him with his eyes, from the top to the bottom.

"Aunty please wait for me over here. I'll be back in a second." said Nikolas and helped her to walk on the pavement so she could wait there. He then went back to the police car.

When he reached the cop's window, a stinky fart smell from inside the police car struck him in the face. The intensity of the smell indicated that the fart must have been distilled through a considerable amount of shit, before it exited the cop's asshole. It was also a very fresh one as Nikolas could almost taste it in his mouth. He was just a breath away from vomiting inside the cop's car, but this would have been a complete disaster. 100% guaranteed.

"I'm sorry for my aunt sir... She's not well after my father died. He was her brother... The doctors gave her strong drugs to help her. But they mess with her head." said Nikolas and turned his head away to take a deep breath with fresh oxygen, clear of the methane from the cop's killer fart. This fart was so strong that it could be the pattern for a biological weapon of massive destruction. Then, he turned his head again towards the cop and, to lighten it up a bit, he added : "Most of the things she says are *apo tin poli erhome ke stin korfi kanela!" (από την πόλη έρχομαι και στην κορφή κανέλλα) [literal translation: from the city I am coming and at the top of the mountain cinnamon. This is a very common Greek phrase that is used to mock the incoherence of speech and the lack of logical order in a discussion].*

What was happening to Nikolas was beyond his wildest imaginations. His heart was racing like a drum and his stomach was about to burst from the cop's rank fart, which he inhaled like a vacuum cleaner.

"So." said the cop with his deep I-can-smell-my-own-stinky-fart-now voice, while looking at him suspiciously with the corner of his eye, and continued: "Where do you go with a school bag on your back on a Sunday morning then?"

"I'm going to my friend Takis to do our homework for tomorrow. We have a test on Religious Education about Jesus Christ's miracles. My favourite one is when he made a blind man see again. What's your favourite miracle Mr Policeman?" asked Nikolas in his most innocent voice possible, trying to hide the fact that he was about to shit his underwear. He also did his best to distract the cop from any further interrogation with this naive question.

"Ok, ok. Just go where you're going little boy. But I'm going to be honest with you. There's something I don't like about you. I don't know what... So go now before I change my mind." said the cop with his I-just-farted-again-run-for-your-life voice.

Nikolas nodded back at him and turned around immediately. He went back to say goodbye to his aunty and rode his bike away like hell.

He felt so pleased with the way he dealt with this complicated scene. He had just managed to dodge a body search from the cops, while carrying one kilo of heroin. He could still hear his heart pounding from the unbelievable stress he went through and his stomach was totally upset from the cop's killer-fart he inhaled.

When he looked at his watch, the excitement was just gone. He could barely make it on time now with all this stupid and extremely risky delay he had experienced.

When he approached the meeting point at the stone slide in the woods, he could see that there were two men already waiting there. One of them was middle aged with a shaved head and the other one, in his mid-twenties, with long hair tied in a ponytail. Nikolas got off his bike and walked towards them.

He realised straight away that the two men were whispering and laughing between them, while they were looking at him. He couldn't hear exactly what they were saying and this undoubtedly pissed him off.

"What's so funny?" he asked them while he was closing on the distance between them.

"What's so funny? What's so funny?" repeated mockingly the older one using a squeaky voice pretending to be a little kid. Then he continued with his normal voice: "You wanna know what's funny little boy? I'll tell you what's funny. What's funny is that we're waiting for a man to show up and a primary pupil appeared with his bike instead. That's what's funny little boy!" Both men burst out laughing with this comment.

Nikolas though, despite being just fourteen years old, was a very tough boy, with an incredibly heavy build for his age. He was also being trained in different martial arts from the very early age of five. On top of that, he was extremely strong in street fights and had gained impeccable skills in using knives, after hanging around with the other fellas from the gang.

The older man walked towards Nikolas. He stopped when he was just a step away and stood right in front of him.

And then he continued provoking him using a high-pitched, feminine tone: "What's this smell? The baby must have pooped his nappy again!" Both doubled over, laughing so hard they could barely breathe.

Nikolas didn't react to any of the insults. All he wanted was to follow the plan he had agreed with Makis; give them the bag he was carrying, take their bag and leave peacefully without any added drama. He was furious though and his patience was already reaching a critical level. His head was burning red, with his nerves about to snap.

"Ignore them.

They're just two idiots.

They don't know you.

They don't know who you really are.

They don't know what you've been through.

Don't speak back to them.

Don't answer to them.

They're so stupid.

Both of them.

Take their bag and go.

Just take the bag and go..." Nikolas thought and kept his mouth shut.

When they stopped laughing, the older man said: "Do you know that your mummy might be looking for you? It's time to breastfeed you little baby!" He then raised his right hand simultaneously, aiming to slap Nikolas on the face.

While the man's hand was fast approaching his left cheek, Nikolas reacted at the speed of light. He took his switchblade out of his back pocket and stabbed the man's palm all the way through. The knife pierced his hand like a spear, with blood exploding out in a shower of red. Before the man even managed to scream from the pain, Nikolas grabbed his head by the hair with a vice-like grip, pulled it lower and gave him a kick with his knee, straight in the nose.

He then moved quickly behind the man, head-locked him with his left hand and by using his right hand, he brought his switchblade half an inch away from the man's right eyeball.

Everything happened in less than four seconds, leaving the younger man unable to react as he was standing there, paralyzed with shock. He never expected a fourteen-year-old boy to be able to destroy his mate, using such high speed and savagery.

"All I wanted was to get the bag! That's all! And now looked what happened! You bastards!" shouted Nikolas angrily to both while he was still chocking the bleeding older man, who was screaming in pain.

Nikolas' eyes were no longer human. They had transformed into the eyes of a predator. He was staring at the younger man, like an angry wolf, ready to attack and kill his pray at any moment.

"Cut it now!" a loud voice was heard.

Three men emerged from the bushes, with two of them holding guns in their hands.

"Drop your knife now and let him go." ordered Andreas, number three in Makis' gang.

Nikolas recognised them and immediately let the screaming and bleeding older man free.

"Give us the bag now." Andreas ordered the younger man, who was still frozen in fear. Apart from what he had witnessed so far, a gun was pointing at his head. He threw the money bag towards Andreas without making a sound.

"You malaka... You think you can insult one of us because of his age? Do you know what'll happen to your tender ass when Makis speaks to your boss about all this shit you pulled out, asshole? Do you? You fuckin bastard?" Andreas asked angrily the older man, who was on his knees in agony holding his bleeding hand, and then gave him a strong kick in the face. When he dropped at his back, Andreas stood next to his bleeding face and said: "Fuck off now son of a bitch. And take your puppy with you. Today's your lucky day. I should have let the boy end you both, you little pussies."

The younger man ran towards the bleeding older man. He helped him to stand up and then, they both disappeared like smoke through the bushes.

"When you choked the old bastard, you had the eyes of the wolf, Nikolas." said Lorenzo the Italian, one of the two men who were there with Andreas. "You're a wolf Nikolas! A real lupo!" he exclaimed.

8:36pm, Thursday 13th May 2010

Lupo combined with Soula in this life-changing event, was like TNT with fire. A wrong decision by Vasilis, would be the spark that could set off a deadly explosion. So huge that could change the lives of different people forever.

For Vasilis it was *'ebros gremos ke piso rema'. (Εμπρός γκρεμός και πίσω ρέμα). [Literal translation: A cliff in the front and a torrent behind. This Greek saying is used when you find yourself between two options that seem equally unpleasant or dangerous no matter which one you end up going for.]*

His brain processed all the factors of this extremely complicated equation and finally reached a decision. Despite all the odds, he would tell Soula the truth about everything. He had his own personal reasons for this.

But before he revealed anything to her, there was a specific term she had to agree with and follow; she would have to swear on Babis' life that the truth would stay with her forever and nobody could ever know anything about it.

"Babis listen carefully. Here is the plan: I'll go back and speak to Soula. My decision is to tell her the truth about what happened. You'll go back to the toilet and check on Tasos. He must go back home and pretend that he's going down with a stomach bug. This way he can stay safe and avoid meeting with Lupo here." said Vasilis with an extremely decisive and authoritarian tone, which suggested no questions of any kind could be asked. Ideally then, Babis would just reply 'No problem, I'll do now.' and after that he would just run to Tasos to the toilets and do as told.

"Are you a malaka? You'll tell mum the truth? Are you stoned? The truth? To mum?" was Babis' response, with his eyes widening in shock and fear.

"I do appreciate where you're coming from. I do. Believe me. But you need to trust me. This is the only way. Right now, we don't have the time to go through the reasons I made this decision. I can explain to you later." said Vasilis.

"And when do you plan to explain your genius decision to me? In Tasos' funeral? Because he'll be in a coffin soon if you tell mum the truth. I'm sure about this because she can't keep her mouth shut. What the hell are you thinking?" asked Babis still quite confused with his older brother's odd decision.

"There're things you don't know about her. And you'll never know. But trust me in one thing; she can keep a secret if she wants to." replied Vasilis.

God will send fire to burn me alive. Do you understand?

"I don't want to go to church today mummy. Please don't make me go there..." Soula, who was about to burst into tears, begged her mother.

"I'm not even discussing about it. Get off your bed, put your clothes on quickly and off you go. Father Alekos is expecting you to be there and help him prepare for the catechism class by 9am. Hurry up and stop complaining. Since last month, every Saturday we have the same discussion with you. This has to stop. Do you understand?" her mother Dina confronted her. She was fed up with Soula's repeated refusal to go to help the one and only priest in their little village.

"But mummy, please... I don't want..."

"Shut it Soula! Do you hear me? Just shut your mouth and get ready. Oh Jesus! Forgive her. She's just young and stupid. That's what she is for not wanting to come to your home and help Father Alekos. This is one of the biggest sins and..." before Dina managed to complete her sentence, little Soula did it for her: "God will send fire and burn me. Isn't it right mummy?"

"Are you making fun of me and Jesus?" Dina screamed and slapped her on the face. "If you say one more word, just one more, I'll tell your father everything and then you'll get the beating you deserve! You little spoilt sinner! Move now! Get up, get dressed, get out of here and go to the church! Now!"

Soula was weeping silently under her hair. It was covering almost all her face as she had slightly bent forwards, after being slapped and bullied by her mother. She was totally horrified to talk back to her. She waited until Dina left the room, so she could change her clothes alone as she felt anxious with the idea of her mother seeing her naked.

She was supposed to meet Father Alekos at the little building next to the church, where he was delivering the Christian Orthodox catechism classes every Saturday morning at 10:30am. All the kids from the village between the ages of six and fifteen years old were attending them religiously. Soula was twelve years old at the time.

Father Alekos was the one and only priest in their village. He had a rather intimidating and scary presence. He had a long black beard and a monstrous face. He weighed over thirty-two stone and was 5ft 4' tall. His voice was excessively frightening, quite deep and booming, making people jump when he spoke. It was so loud that he never had to use microphones and speakers during the Sunday service in a church full of believers (or non-believers).

Rumours had it that he had a criminal past and had spent some years in prison when he was younger. Nobody in the village was aware of the exact crimes he had committed or any other details about his offences, because nobody knew him when he was young. He came from the north of Greece and was appointed as a priest in this village about a decade ago. Since he was a member of the Greek Orthodox Church, no-one in the village could challenge his validity and authority. Only the courageous villagers used to say behind his back that *'I putana san yerasi, yinete kaloyria'. (Η πουτάνα σαν γεράσει γίνεται καλόγρια.) [literal translation: When the prostitute gets old, she becomes a nun. This phrase is self-explanatory in Father Alekos' case.]*

This man was a vile one and wasn't a close friend with water. He had a personal hygiene routine straight from the Victorian times and smelled of booze all day – every day. The result was that, at the end of his second week without any shower, he smelled worse than a durian. This is a fruit native to Southeast Asia, with an odour that has been described as turpentine, rotten onions, and sewage. This fruit is so smelly that it had been banned on public transport in Singapore and Thailand.

But on the contrary, Father Alekos wasn't banned from anywhere. He could move freely around the village leaving his reeking body odour behind him like a ferret does, when marking his territory. If someone needed to find him quickly, all they had to do was to use their nostrils and follow his stinking smell, which could remain in the air longer than the smell of common human shit.

The two week-mark with no shower was usually the milestone for him. That was when his wife, Marika, would help her husband, to have a proper shower and get rid of his trademark durian smell.

Little Soula was twenty-five minutes late when she finally arrived at the little building next to the church. The last few Saturdays, she was taking her time to get there. She felt that the less time she spent with this disgusting beast, the better. Father Alekos was making her feel extremely uncomfortable, especially with some of his comments about her body. Also, she couldn't stand his stinky smell after a point. Therefore, she would walk at a very slow pace and use a longer route to get there, ending up spending over twenty minutes each time, for a five to six minutes' walk.

Father Alekos was sitting on his high back wing chair, made from real black leather. It was a grandiose piece of furniture with two dominating double-headed eagles in both sides at the top of the back. He had almost finished his breakfast, a 200ml bottle of Ouzo to kick off the day. When he saw Soula entering the room, he raised the bottle with the Ouzo and drank whatever was left in it. This was his usual breakfast; plain Ouzo in room temperature. The authentic breakfast of a Greek alcoholic.

"You're late. Again. Last Saturday the same. And the one before. This time I'll speak to your father. That's it." Father Alekos warned her angrily with his deep, scary and semi-drunk voice.

"No Father, no! Please! Don't! Don't say anything to my dad! Please!" Soula begged him. She was horrified even with the thought of her father receiving a complaint about her continuous lateness from God's representative in their village.

Apart from the beatings, there was a variety of other punishments she could receive from him, depending on the seriousness of her sin each time. This included being locked in her room for a full day or more, with no books or radio or any other human contact. In 1967, TV or phones were not even in play yet, in their small village in Central Greece.

Experiencing unreasonable punishment and physical abuse had already happened so many times in the past as her father was mentally unstable. He pretended to be a well-behaved, civilised, law-abiding Orthodox Christian to all people outside his family. But with the members of his close family, he would turn into an abusive, rude, ill-mannered, high-tempered and violent piece of shit, who would physically and mentally abuse Soula, her mother and two younger sisters, at every given opportunity.

With only a few exemptions, the majority of the men in their village were pretty much behaving in a similar way towards their families. This was not limited to their small village; in the entirety of Greece, including the larger cities, it was socially acceptable to be an asshole to your wife and kids.

Her father was close mates and drinking buddies with Father Aleko. This meant that whatever bullshit this beast of a priest told him about Soula, he would accept it de facto, without even checking her side of the story.

"Well... I don't know... It's very difficult for me not to reveal the truth to your father. You see, I am God's representative on this earth. I cannot hide the truth from His believers. God will send fire to burn me alive. Do you understand?" explained Father Alecos, staring into her eyes as if he was trying to hypnotise her.

"Yes! I do! I understand! Really! I do! But please don't say anything to my dad! Please!" Soula begged him for one more time. She was now sobbing uncontrollably.

"Do you have a boyfriend? Is this why you're late every Saturday? This is it! I knew it! Your father needs to know everything about it and I'll make sure I'll tell him, when I see him in the taverna later." he threatened her in a very persuasive and intimidating manner.

Twelve-year-old Soula's interactions with boys were only limited to ball games in the village square and during the breaks between classes in school.

"Oh my god!!... I never Father!!... I never!! I..." little Soula sobbed so hard that that she couldn't even finish her sentence.

"I don't believe you. You must prove it to me." he said strictly.

"I will do... anything you ask me... Father! Please... don't say anything to my dad!! Please!!" she kept begging him with her whole body shaking, while looking straight into his eyes.

"Well. Stop crying now. There's something we can do about it. Do you want me to tell you what?" he asked her, expecting only a yes for an answer.

"Yes Father!! Yes!! And I'll do anything you ask me to prove that I don't have a boyfriend!" little Soula agreed and almost stopped crying. A spark of hope flashed in her eyes, a sign that she might finally escape from the nasty position she found herself in.

"Ok. You know I'm God's messenger on earth. Don't you?" he asked her.

"Yes father. I do."

"Ok then. When a big girl like you wants to prove to a priest like me that she has no boyfriend, so the priest doesn't say anything about it to her father, God has asked us to make some checks on the girl. This will help God see that everything is clear and nothing has happened with a boyfriend. Are you ok with me to check what God needs to see?" he asked little Soula, still sitting on his chair, from which he hadn't move an inch all this time.

"I'm ok Father... I'm ok..." she insisted, but her eyes betrayed her fear. She knew that Father Alekos was up to something, but she didn't have the power to stop him.

"Come closer then and stand in front of me."

Soula just followed his order. She moved forward so her legs were almost touching his knees and her head was in straight line with his head.

"Now, turn around and bend over so I can do the checks." he ordered her again and a foul-smelling breath blasted her in the face. It was a combination of garlic, rotten teeth not washed for weeks, red onions, tobacco and Ouzo. This reeking smell forced her to turn around and bend over, faster than her shadow.

Father Alekos finally found a serious reason to move his enormous body, which was stuck in the sacred leather high back wing chair. In order to be able to reach Soula, he opened his knees and fitted his swollen belly between his thighs.

As Soula had bent over, he lifted her skirt with his left hand and with the right one, he quickly lowered her underwear. Then with his chubby fingers, he moved towards her private parts and made a scary noise similar to a big gorilla ejaculating.

Nooo!! Stop it!!" Nooo!!! Soula screamed and jumped forward, falling on her knees and then onto the floor. "What is this?? What are you doing??" she continued screaming while she was still on the floor, trying to lift her underwear.

Father Alekos sprang out of his sacred chair, moved next to Soula's face and gave her a strong slap.

"You little bitch! You're done! You have no idea what I'll say to your father now!" he roared in anger and stormed out of the room.

Little Soula, in absolute shock and with tears streaming down her face again, stood up and ran so she could reach him. If Father Alekos spoke to her dad, she feared for her life. Literally.

When she stepped out of the room, she saw him in the distance, preparing to descend the stairs, which would take him down from the churchyard and onto the road. The stairs were steep and daunting, with about sixty steps and two landings along the way.

The exact moment Father Alekos lifted his right leg to

descend the stairs, Soula shouted at him: "Noooo Father!! Waaaiiiit!!"

Out of instinct, he turned his head towards Soula's direction. This made him miscalculate his first step down the stairs. As a result, he tripped over and started rolling down the steep steps, the same way a wine barrel would roll down a hill with forty-five-degree slope.

The fact that he was semi-drunk and had already gained strong momentum before he reached the first step, resulted in him rolling down the entire set of the sixty steps. Even the two landings in between were not enough to stop him. His body came to a sudden and violent stop at the iron gate, which clanged loudly as it hit on it.

Soula was shocked to her bones. Her whole body was shacking like she was being electrocuted. After the moment she shouted at him to hold on and wait, she completely lost him from her sight. She could only hear him screaming as he was rolling down the stairs.

Seconds after, when her head communicated again with the environment around her, she ran towards the edge of the stairs, to see what exactly had happened to Father Alekos.

What she came across scarred her for life; the stairs were full of blood stains all the way down. At the very bottom, Father Alekos' body was lying motionless in a pool of blood on the concrete ground around him.

"The beast is dead..." she thought.

Apart from his wife, nobody else in the small village was truly bothered by this outcome, as Father Alekos wasn't the best role model for an Orthodox Christian audience. Nobody would openly admit it, but the village was undoubtedly relieved from his early and sudden death, in the same way you are relieved when you get rid of a nasty haemorrhoid.

The next priest who replaced him was the complete opposite.

A decent, fit and healthy young man with a beautiful wife and two very young daughters. He was living and breathing the Orthodox Christianity values at every given opportunity. He didn't drink, never smoked in his life and was very well mannered. Everyone in the village loved him straight away, which made it very easy for them to forget about Father Alekos very quickly. The only ones who would remember him every now and then, were his drinking buddies, but even them, they preferred the new priest-version to lead their church, who didn't smell like a durian as well.

Without realising it, Soula had done a massive favour to her village. The issue, however, was that she exclusively blamed herself for his death. This guilt was so severe that she felt she had lost a part of herself. She was a deeply religious girl who had always believed in God and in the power of prayer. But after this accident, her faith in Christianity was fortified. This was her own way of fighting another guilt; the one that part of herself enjoyed seeing this vile human being dive to his own death. Therefore, she prayed more than ever before and went to church every day. She also focused on reading the Bible and learning more about her religion, which formulated her future personality as an adult.

Soula never revealed what happened that morning between her and Father Alekos to anyone. Apart from one person.

In 2000, a year after her husband Ilias died from a heart attack, she shared this life-changing experience with her oldest son Vasilis.

8:39pm, Thursday 13th May 2010

"How can you be so sure? I don't understand. It doesn't make any sense to me. I think it's completely stupid to tell the truth to mum." Babis continued showing his disbelief by just criticising and challenging his brother's decision, and like always, without suggesting something instead.

"Ok Babis. Ok. This is how the story goes. My car is parked at the front of the taverna. In less than a minute, I'll be there from the back door. I don't even have to go back inside to see Soula. And then I'll drive home. Anyway, the tasks I have to complete can easily wait until tomorrow or even better, the day after tomorrow. This means that you'll have to go back inside and sort everything out with everyone all by yourself. This also means that you'll be able to make the right decisions freely, without my 'stupid' interference. To be frankly honest, this isn't my mess bro. I can easily turn my mode to NSG." Vasilis responded in a relatively calm tone.

"What's this NSG now?" asked Babis.

"No Shit Given. That's what NSG means little bro." replied Vasilis and walked towards the back exit where his car was parked.

Babis could easily do with a piece of adult nappies. He almost shat himself when he heard Vasilis' response and saw him walking away from him. To prevent Vasilis from taking another step, he acted rapidly. He jumped like a chimpanzee and grabbed Vasilis by both shoulders.

"Stop Vasilis! Stop! I take it back! You're right! I agree! This is what we need to do! That's the only way! I agree!" shouted Babis after he managed to immobilise his brother, with his magnificent jump.

In reality, he didn't believe this was the right way to go forward though. But the lack of any other proposal from his side and the threat from Vasilis to abandon him, gave him no other choice than to finally surrender and accept his older brother's plan.

Vasilis bluffed Babis with his threat to leave him in the absolute shit. He knew very well that Babis had no actual working suggestion of what to do, so he would finally follow whatever he decided.

"Alright Babis. From this point, just follow my lead. I have a plan in my head and I believe it will work. But I need you to be on my side and not go against my decisions like you do all the time. Otherwise, let's split now, malaka. Are you with me?"

"Yes. I am." Babis answered with his ego deeply wounded.

"Perfect. I'll go speak to Soula. You go check with Tasos at the toilets. I hope he's still there."

When they re-entered the bar area, Babis went straight to the toilets, without making any eye-contact with Soula to avoid any questions from her. She was standing behind the bar, waiting impatiently to interrogate any of her sons.

Vasilis, who followed him, went straight to the bar and sat at a bar-stool in front of her. She was just by herself. None of her nosy friends were around, so the conditions were the right ones to explain to her what had happened.

"Welcome back my love! You know very well that I believe you're a clever boy. So you must already know I have a couple of questions to ask you about Tasos. He's in the toilets since he came into the taverna in panic. And please, don't tell me he's there trying to recover from the glass that landed on his head after they crashed with my Babis, because I'm not having it." declared Soula staring into his eyes, trying to identify any tell-tale signs, if he was going to lie to her.

"Listen to me carefully Soula. You have to swear on Babis' life that whatever I tell you, will stay with you forever and nobody will ever know anything about it. And I mean it. With you and only you forever. If you feel that you can't do this, I'll tell you nothing and you'll never find out what has actually happened. Babis and Tasos won't tell you anything and never answer any of your questions unless you swear to me." Now it was his turn to stare into her eyes, to realise if she was willing to be totally honest with him.

"I knew it! I knew it! Something's wrong! From the way Tasos was looking around when he came in here! He was looking for my Babis! Oh my God! Oh my God! Oh my God! What has happened Vasilis? Is my Babis in danger? Is someone looking for him? Did he say to his girlfriend that he loves her and that he will marry her and then left her and now her family is looking for him and Tasos came here to warn him? Did he get her pregnant and then left her and now her angry father's searching for him and Tasos wanted to tell him to hide? Vasilis, please tell me what happened to my Babis!"

Without a doubt, Vasilis didn't expect a calmer reaction than this one from Soula. He was already mentally prepared to move to the next stage of their conversation, after this initial explosion.

"If you don't calm down now, lower your voice and stop asking me one thousand questions per millisecond, believe me, I'll tell you nothing." Vasilis warned her in a very confrontational tone.

"Ok, ok, I'll calm down and try to stop the questions." Soula's voice dropped to a near-whisper as she replied.

"Try isn't good enough Soula. I need you to stop the questions altogether. Not just try."

"I will stop them, I promise. Just one last question. Please, just one. Is my Babis in danger? Tell me, is he?"

"No. Your Babis is not in any kind of danger. This has nothing to do with your Babis. OK now?"

"Thank you God! Thank you! I know You are always protecting me and all my family, from Your Kingdom up in the skies!" exclaimed Soula, while she performed the sign of the cross on herself looking towards the ceiling, as she was speaking directly to the Creator, the Almighty Himself.

"And now that you know your Babis isn't in any danger, do you swear on his life that the truth will stay with you forever and nobody could ever know anything about it?"

"I swear." she answered.

"This is not enough. Say *I swear on Babis' life.*" demanded Vasilis.

"Oooohh! How difficult can you be sometimes... I swear on Babis' life. There you go. Are you happy? Tell me everything now!" said Soula.

"And before I tell you what happened, you need to promise me one more thing; you won't start firing questions at me, because I don't know every little detail of the story. Do you promise me this Soula?" asked Vasilis expecting only a 'Yes, I promise you.' as an answer.

"Yes, I promise you, I won't! Please tell me everything now! Don't keep me waiting! Can't you see I'm dying to hear what has happened?" Soula was looking at him with her eyes so wide open that they looked like they were ready to pop out of her eye sockets.

"Ok. Here we go. Tasos, who's a bit drunk, had sex with Barbara on a bench at the park almost half an hour ago. He also had a small accident and that's why he is stuck in the toilets. All I wan…"

"What?? Can you say that again? What?" she almost shouted as she couldn't believe in her ears. The promise she gave seconds ago not to ask any questions was already broken.

"It's exactly what I just said: Tasos, who's a bit drunk, had sex with Barbara on a bench at the park almost half an hour ago. I know it sounds craz…"

"Oh. My. God!" She paused completely, staring into his eyes without actually seeing him. She kept staring at him, entirely transfixed, as if he had cast a magic spell on her.

Vasilis opened his mouth to say something and, before his voice managed to escape his larynx, she returned from the outer space she had been, and started again.

"What a sin! What a sin! Barbara is a married woman! She is a mother! Her son Lakis is best friends with Tasos and my little Babis! And today is her twenty-fifth wedding anniversary with Nikolas!... "

And before she managed to make her next exclamation statement...

BOOM!!

Lupo appeared in front of them.

Just by himself. Without Barbara or Lakis.

So focused were they on each other, they didn't see Lupo come barging in the taverna. He had scanned all the customer tables with his extremely wild eyes, looking for someone. When he didn't find what he was looking for, he headed straight for the bar, where mother and son were located, completely oblivious to his arrival.

Soula's eyes widened in shock as she saw Lupo standing in front of her. She felt her heart skip a beat and she almost jumped from her position. She rose to her feet and opened her mouth to speak, but the words died on her lips. She felt a wave of dizziness wash over her and then everything went black. She collapsed unconscious to the floor behind the bar.

"Oh fuck! Is she ok? What happened to her?" asked Lupo and ran inside the bar.

"I'm not sure. She was telling me about the day my father died and probably this memory made her faint..." answered Vasilis without a second thought and any delay, while he leaned over to help his unconscious mother.

I can only see four here mate...

"What you have, Ilias is ACS or acute coronary syndrome, as we doctors, call it. This describes a range of conditions associated with sudden and reduced blood flow to the heart. In your case, I can say you're lucky because it was a mild heart attack. All these symptoms you had, like the discomfort in your chest that went away and came back, accompanied with uncomfortable pressure and feeling light-headed, ready to faint, are the exact ones of a heart attack. If you experience them again, call an ambulance immediately. You need to come straight to the hospital. I'll prescribe you these tablets. At first, you need to take 300 milligrams of them, which are four 75 mg tablets as a single dose. Then, a maintenance dose of one 75 mg tablet once a day. Follow this, until our next appointment in two weeks. And, as I already told you, no more smoking and drinking. At all. You need to follow the diet we gave you as well. Unless you want to die young and leave your wife and kids on their own. Any questions?" asked Dr Titkas, one of the Consultant Cardiologists of the public hospital.

"No questions doctor. You said it all. When can I go back home?" asked Ilias from his bed, with Soula sitting patiently next to him.

"Your paperwork should be ready in half an hour. When everything is completed, the nurses will let you know and then you can go." answered the doctor.

"Thank you doctor! Thank you so much for keeping my husband alive!" said Soula and stood up from her chair. She then walked towards Dr Titkas. She took a white envelope out of her purse and put it in the doctor's uniform pocket. It was a *'fakelaki'* (bribe in Greek), with one hundred thousand Greek Drachmas in it.

Dr Titkas took it and put it in one of his internal pockets. He then turned around and left the room at once, without saying a word.

Ilias waited until the doctor left the room and said: "The scumbag! We had to pay him all this extra money to do his job! Isn't this malaka getting paid a salary each month? He's a civil servant, isn't he? When my friend Kostas visited me here yesterday, told me everything about him. This Titkas is a greedy bastard. He's taking advantage of people's pain and has made a bloody fortune from their misery. He owns over ten houses and flats, and he lives like a king with his doctor wife, in their mansion with the two pools and tennis court..."

"If we didn't pay him, you could still be waiting out there, for a doctor to see you. Which means that you could have been dead now, so stop complaining. Anyway, most of the doctors in the hospitals ask for their *'fakelaki'* to make things go faster. If you don't pay, you must pray to God for a miracle. Didn't you know this already?" Soula tried to put him back in order.

"That's why they're all rich. How can a doctor from a public hospital buy all these properties, with just a salary ? How can he own two sport cars, one 4x4 and a limo?" wondered Ilias, full of anger. And then he continued: "That's why I always said to our Vasilis to become a doctor, but he never listened to me..."

"It is what it is. We can't change the Greek system. It will never change, I believe. We're in Easter 1999 now. We'll have the same discussion in Easter 2019. So come on now, get up. We're going home and you're alive. This is what you need to remember and forget about the money we paid Titkas." said Soula and helped him stand up from his bed.

When they returned to their flat, all the family gathered at the kitchen table to discuss what had happened. They also explained to Vasilis and Babis, all the necessary information about Ilias' medication and where it would be stored. Finally, they informed the two boys about what to do, in case he experienced another heart attack and they were alone with him.

The little container in a cylinder shape with the orange-pink tablets would be kept in a drawer in the kitchen, to allow easy access for everyone. The rest of his medication and other drugs were kept there too.

Vasilis fell immediately in love with the little container with the orange-pink tablets. It gave him a brilliant idea; he could use the empty ones to store the Ecstasy pills he was occasionally selling. This way, if he was stopped and searched by the cops, he could claim that this was his father's medication. The containers already had a sticker from the pharmacy with the instructions on them anyway.

The perfect cover he thought...

Vasilis was nineteen years old and deeply into recreational drugs during the last year. Apart from smoking weed and occasionally swallowing Ecstasy pills in underground parties with electronic music, he was also selling small quantities to 'friends', to support his partying lifestyle.

He left his family home when he turned eighteen and had been living by himself in the city centre of Athens ever since. He was renting a small studio apartment and worked as a bartender in one the biggest underground nightclubs in the city centre, owned by Lupo. He was only visiting his family for a limited number of days each time, during Christmas, Easter and summer.

In July 1999, Vasilis had returned at his family home for a week , just before his scheduled summer holidays. He had made mega-holiday plans with his four best mates as they were planning to spend two full weeks in three different Greek Islands. They would start with Paros, then Ios and complete their tour in Mykonos. Their plan was to party like animals, based on the fact that this was their first ever holiday in the Greek islands as adults, without any members of their families.

As always, Vasilis needed the extra funds to cover his two-week holiday. His father, *Ilias the Tight-fisted Prick*, who was managing the family budget, wouldn't give him the full amount he was asking for. So, the solution to this problem was to 'push some gear to get the extra cash in'.

His plan was to sell one hundred and fifty high-quality Ecstasy pills at an increased price, to a specific person he knew, who was loaded with money and only cared about quality. These specific pills were also in pink-orange colour and after a 'test drive' he had with them, he was super confident about their top quality and extraordinary strength. One of them had almost the same effect as three average quality Ecstasy pills. This meant only one thing in his brain; he could easily sell them to the loaded guy at a price five times higher than normal and make some strong cash for his adventure in the Greek Islands.

The buyer was located approximately ninety minutes away from his flat, if he used the city public buses and the traffic was normal. At least, this guy lived in a posh area in Athens. So, Vasilis didn't have to go to a shithole place, where he would have to check behind his back all the time either not to get robbed by the local gangs or stopped by undercover cops.

His master-plan to carry the Ecstasy pills was based on using the empty containers. He would use five of them with thirty pills in each. Then he would put the containers in a paper bag from the pharmacy they were buying them from.

To play completely safe, he would also 'borrow' his father's health booklet and carry it inside the bag with the 'E's. This way, he could claim he was returning from the pharmacy with his father's medication for his very sensitive and aching heart. He would also be dressed like a good Christian boy going to church for the Sunday service. No earrings, no sunglasses, hair tied in a neat ponytail. Just like a well-behaved boy going to church to pray to God.

The day to do the deal had arrived. It was set for 1pm on Saturday 17th July, just a week before the holidays with his mates. He was home alone and the time was around 10am. Ilias, Soula and Babis had left half an hour ago to go to the supermarket for the weekly shopping. He didn't expect anyone to come back within the following hour at least.

After everyone left, Vasilis dressed, as planned, like a proper Christian boy going to Sunday service. He would then do all the prep for the deal on the kitchen table. It had all the space he needed to complete the counts without missing a beat.

He then turned on progressive trance music, with the volume set almost to the maximum, to provide him with the rhythm he needed to complete the job. He split the 'E's in five containers, exactly thirty in each. He then placed the containers on the table and according to his plan, he would put them in the paper bag from the pharmacy just before he left the flat.

He thought that if he quickly smoked a very small spliff outside, at the balcony of the living room, it would help him take a load off his head. He was already under high pressure to complete this deal smoothly, without any complications.

Therefore, he took swift action. He rolled a single joint from the strong Kalamata weed he had in stock for the Greek islands' holiday and went outside to light it up. He had made the joint a bit strong to last him for the following hours, as he had to travel relatively far to meet the buyer.

Like always, the joint was a bit stronger than he was aiming for. The result was that he got extremely stoned very quickly and *'ithe to Hristo fadaro'. (είδε το Χριστό φαντάρο) [literal translation: He saw Christ as a soldier. This phrase has multiple applications in the Greek slang, and one of them is to describe someone stoned to the bone, so high they can see Jesus dressed as a Marine Corps soldier in front of them.]*

 When he had almost finished the joint and was high as a kite, a shock of reality hit him like a thunderclap; he saw his family's car, with everyone inside, pulling into their car park.

"No! No! No! What the hell? Why're they back so soon?" he asked his stoned self out-loud and rushed back inside.

He stopped the music and ran quickly to the kitchen. He took the air freshener from the cupboard under the sink and sprayed all the rooms in the flat. But the joint had freaked him out, making him think that the smell from the weed was still everywhere inside the flat. To resolve this, he ran around the rooms and opened all the balcony doors and windows, to create an air stream that could clear the smell.

When he finished, while he was rushing back to the kitchen, the doorbell rang. He ignored it and went straight to the kitchen. He held the paper bag from the pharmacy with one hand and with the other, he tried to grab all the five containers .

Being so stoned didn't really help him to complete this task successfully. All the containers slipped his hands and fell on the floor. But he was quite lucky in his unluckiness. They fell on the carpet and stayed closed with their lids on, keeping all the pills inside them. While he tried to pick them up, he heard the sound of keys turning the lock and the main door of the flat opening.

He quickly picked all the containers from the floor, dropped them in the paper bag and ran out of the kitchen, towards the toilet, like hell. Ilias, Soula and Babis were already inside the flat and saw him entering the toilet like he had a severe diarrhoea attack. They all looked at each other and continued walking.

Vasilis locked himself in there and faked noises, pretending that he was having a tricky shit. Soula went outside the toilet door and asked: "Are you ok?"

"I'm ok. Just having a number two. Why are you back so early? What happened?" he asked from inside the toilet, with the door still locked.

"Your father didn't feel well and we had to bring him back home. Can you stay with him until I return from the supermarket? I'll take Babis with me to help me." Soula asked him, still standing outside the toilet.

"I can't. I have a date and I'm already late. Babis will have to stay with him." he answered.

"I hope your date worth's it. I have to leave now, I'm running late. See you at lunch." said Soula and left home to go shopping just by herself.

Vasilis waited inside the toilet, until he heard the main door opening and closing, to ensure that Soula had definitely left. In the meantime, *'Ilias the Not-Feeling-So-Well Prick'* had already gone to his bedroom to rest.

When he was certain that Soula had departed, he got out of the toilet, still stoned but not as chilled as he thought he would be at this point in time. He was holding the paper bag in his hands and went straight to the main door to leave their flat as soon as possible.

His target was to disappear from there without speaking to anyone. When he passed the kitchen, he saw with the corner of his eye, Babis, in front of the fridge with the door open, holding a slice of ham in the air, ready to land it inside his fully open mouth. He continued straight without saying a word. He was finally outside the flat, but without his father's Health booklet, as he had originally planned.

The joint he smoked was so strong, it was still kicking in. Even after this highly dampening experience, he wasn't coming down, even to the slightest degree.

"That was a close one.

What the shit happened there?

I hope it doesn't smell weed in the flat.

I opened all the stupid doors.

And all the windows.

It shouldn't smell.

But if it is?

Ilias the Mega Prick will try to kill me.

I need to be ready for his attack when I return.

He'll be fuming.

I'm sure.

He'll call me all the names he knows.

And he'll try to smack me.

But I won't let him.

I can take his old ass down.

Easy..." he thought as he started his trip with the bus.

After almost two hours, due to the heavy traffic at different points in Athens, he managed to arrive at the buyer's house. He was just on time for their appointment at 1pm. The house was a mansion with a high wall surrounding it and he was instructed to just ring the bell when he arrived. The buyer answered through the telecom system and instructed Vasilis to turn straight left, after he entered the property and go to the wooden garden room, where he was waiting for him.

"Alo Vasilis! How's everything bro?" asked Spyros, the buyer.

"All good, Spyros! All good my friend! Can't wait for next Friday. We're going on a two-week holiday in Paros, Ios and then Mykonos! We're going to get smashed mate!" answer Vasilis who was still stoned.

"Sounds great my mate! I'm also going to Mykonos for three weeks at the start of August! We all need to meet there and have a drink, if you know what I mean! So, what do you have for me here?" asked Spyros.

"This 'E' is another level man! One of them is as strong as three normal ones! You won't believe it!" replied Vasilis with pure excitement.

"Oh man! I can't wait to try them tonight! We're having a private party here with a few good people and you're invited, if you're free."

"Thank you bro, but I have plans for tonight. Anyways, here you are mate." said Vasilis and passed the pharmacy paper bag to Spyros.

"Are these one-fifty?" asked Spyros when he looked inside the bag.

"Yes. One hundred and fifty exactly. Five containers. Thirty in each." answered Vasilis fully confident about his counts.

"I can only see four here mate..." said Spyros a bit annoyed.

"What're you talking about?? Let me see!!" Vasilis answered and grabbed the paper bag back at the same time. When he looked inside it, he froze for four seconds with his eyes wide open.

"What the fuck?? What the fuck?? What the absolute fuck?? Where's the fifth? What the fuck?? I had five of them!!" Vasilis couldn't explain what had happened. He certainly had five containers on the kitchen table. 100% certain.

"So, if there's thirty in each one, does this mean you only brought one-twenty? I'm not happy with it man... Not happy at all..." said Spyros overly frustrated and then continued: "I've made promises to people. And now, I will let them down. You get this. Do you?"

Vasilis was lost for words. He didn't know how to truly feel or respond to him.

"I do mate... I do. But I can't understand what happened. When I left my place, I had five of them. I'm 100% sure." said Vasilis, without including the fact that he was also completely doped when he left his flat...

"Ok. Ok Vasilis. What will happen now is that I will pay you for one hundred and ten. The ten is my compensation for all this. Ok?"

"I'm devastated mate. I'm so sorry, honestly. I'm ok with one-ten, yes. It's my mistake anyway..." said Vasilis and took the money from Spyros.

The fifth container haunted him for two hours on his way back. His stoned brain couldn't come up with a reasonable explanation for its disappearance.

When he finally arrived home, it was around 3:30pm, well past his family lunch time. He soon realised that something wasn't right. When he reached the main door of their flat, it was extremely quiet inside. Usually, the TV was playing at such volume that it could be clearly heard when you got out of the elevator, which was fifty feet away from the main entrance to their flat.

He opened the door and nobody was in the living room.

There was a deadly silence in the flat. He walked towards the kitchen, still no sign of anyone. He thought that they might be all taking a nap, which was a bit unusual. So, he restrained himself from calling out their names just in case he woke them up.

He then walked into his bedroom. Babis was lying on his bed with his face down. As he approached him, he realised that he was silently crying.

"What's going on? Why are you crying? And why are you alone? Where's the rest?" asked Vasilis and sat on the bed next to his brother.

"Dad... isn't well! I'm... so scared!" replied Babis and began sobbing.

"Just take some good deep breaths and tell me slowly what happened after you came back home in the morning. Step by step." said calmly to his overwhelmed brother, to help him stop crying.

Babis started explaining what had happened while crying at the same time. "Dad didn't feel well when we went to the supermarket... And then we came back home... And Mum left to go to the supermarket... And she asked me to stay with him because you had to go somewhere... Then dad went to his bedroom... And he asked me to get him one of his pills from the kitchen drawer... And I went to the kitchen... And I found a container with his pills on the floor... and I took out one pill from it and gave it to him..."

Vasilis got petrified.

His heart was beating so fast that it felt like it was going to burst out of his chest, with his pulse exceeding two hundred beats per minute. A grave disaster had just probably happened...

"Stand still Babis! Don't move! I'll be back in a second!"

He jumped off the bed, got out of his bedroom and ran to the kitchen faster than sound. He went straight to the drawer, where they kept his father's pills.

When he opened the drawer, the first thing he saw was Spyros' missing fifth container with the 'E's...

Time came to a halt.

His brain couldn't process the information received from his eyes. *'lias the Heart-Aching Prick'* must have taken one of the strongest Ecstasy pills in the market without knowing it...

"Keep calm malaka!

Keep calm!

Keep yourself together!

Whatever happened, happened.

You didn't do anything on purpose.

Always remember this!

Go back to Babis.

Ask him what happened next.

Like you have no clue.

And take the 'E's out of the drawer!!!

Go!

Now!" his inner voice instructed him. Without these instructions, he would still be standing there, looking at the container with the Ecstasy pills, which had probably destroyed his father.

"All good Babis! Tell me what happened next." he said when he returned at the bedroom after a couple of minutes, pretending that everything was normal.

Babis continued to explain what had happened, even as the tears streamed down his face. He hadn't moved an inch from where Vasilis had left him. "Then I went to the living room... to play video games and after a bit... I heard dad shouting from his bedroom... And then I got up to go see what he wanted and then... I saw him outside his bedroom... And he took two steps and he fell on the floor..." Babis let out a loud, wailing sob that sounded like a new-born crying.

Vasilis moved closer to him and hugged him firmly with both

of his hands. He allowed him to cry for as long as he needed. He was crying as well as he knew that this wouldn't have a happy ending for their father.

When Babis stopped crying uncontrollably, Vasilis asked him what happened after their father collapsed on the floor. Babis explained that he didn't know what to do and was totally scared because he wasn't responding at all. He kept shouting at him, but nothing. He then said that he went and knocked the door of the flat next to theirs and Ria, who leaves there, came over to see what had happened. She called an ambulance, which came relatively quickly and took Ilias to the hospital. He also explained when Soula returned from the supermarket and they told her what had happened, she left straight for the hospital. Before she left, she asked Ria to keep an eye on Babis. She agreed with it and if he needed anything until Vasilis returned, he could knock at her door.

It was exactly 1:01pm on Saturday 17th July 1999, when Ilias was pronounced dead from a heavy heart attack, on his way to the hospital.

The medics never performed an autopsy or any further investigation to determine the actual cause of his death. They all believed that his history of heart conditions was the reason for his heart attack.

Vasilis' life took a sharp turn after his father's accidental death, as he couldn't shake the guilt, knowing his irresponsible actions and reckless choices caused his death. His decision was to keep this secret locked away, never telling anyone. But this secret burdened him as he couldn't find the courage to share it with anyone.

In the days following Ilias' death, he experienced a profound and overwhelming shock. It felt like he was hit by a freight train and left in a state of disbelief and despair. He was unable to understand what he was actually going through.

The most direct impact was to withdraw from the world around him. He didn't even answer the phone to his three best friends whenever they tried calling to offer him support. Vasilis had built an impenetrable wall around himself, shutting out everyone and everything from the outside world.

Each morning was a battle with the grief and he found it nearly impossible to get out of bed. The vibrant colours of his life not so many days before, when he was getting ready for the summer holidays in the Greek Islands with his best friends, had faded to grayscale, with everything feeling heavy and meaningless now. Depression led him feeling trapped in a never-ending cycle of sadness and despair. In those early days, knowing that his Ecstasy pills had led to his father's death resulted in all-consuming guilt, followed by deep grief.

In the months that followed, after he managed to face the darkness within himself, fight his inner demons and recognise the weight of his actions, Vasilis had a life-changing moment of clarity. He made a promise never to touch any kind of drugs again, as a tribute to his late father and a commitment to living responsibly.

This catharsis was the main factor for this astonishing turn in his life. Though he couldn't change the past and all the nastiness between him and Ilias, he aimed to build a future that honoured the positives from his father's life and allowed him to find peace within himself. The guilt he felt at first turned into a strong motivation for a fresh start and making things right in the future.

8:48pm, Thursday 13th May 2010

"We must take her to the storage room in the back now! Before the customers see her 'lifeless' body on the floor and spread panic in the taverna. There's a bed there we can use. Let me quickly get Babis to give us a hand. Please stay with her and I'll be right back." Vasilis asked Lupo in the best possible way he could not to raise any suspicions with him.

He then went straight to the toilets to find Babis. Lupo tried to revive Soula by giving her gentle face slaps and calling her name on repeat, without any result. She was lying motionless on the floor, but at least, she was still breathing.

In order not to blow up Tasos' hiding place, Vasilis opened the toilet door and said: "Babis, we need you out here right now. Soula isn't well. You need to come now!"

He stood poised by the door, anticipating Babis' exit from the toilet cabinet where Tasos was kept hidden. When Vasilis saw him, he blinked and placed his right index finger on his lips, sending him a signal to keep his mouth shut for something he couldn't explain at that specific moment.

Despite his usual resistance to Vasilis' requests, Babis surprisingly remained calm and quietly obeyed, without saying a word. It was just after he exited the toilets and saw Lupo trying to revive his motionless mum lying on the floor, when he freaked out.

Vasilis shot a quick look at Babis. What he saw was his brother's colossal head sweating like a waterfall, while his throat seemed to wrestle with swallowing a ping pong ball coated in sand.

While Lupo was still busy trying to revive Soula, Vasilis grabbed Babis' hand and looked at him in the eyes. He then blinked and made a move with his head to follow him. The translation to this message was: *'Don't worry. I'll deal with this. Just follow me and keep your mouth shut, unless you're asked something directly.'*

It wasn't quite certain that Babis' brain matched this translation though.

So this makes you a winner Vasilis??

Three weeks before his father was officially declared dead, Vasilis had returned to his family home in Athens. It was 5:45pm on the 25th June 1999, a hot Friday with scorching temperatures reaching 38°C (100.4°F). Him and his best friends were in their favourite coffee-bar, getting pissed in the middle of the day.

"Well, I have a small surprise for you boys." Vasilis informed his mates, who all stopped talking to each other to listen to his announcement.

He looked at them with a cheeky smile, pulled a tinny bag out of his pocket and placed it discreetly on their table.

"My man!" exclaimed Antonis, one of his mates. "You did your magic again! Smashing bro!" he continued and hi-fived Vasilis.

"Where's it from? Is it good" asked Louis, the third member of the gang.

"My guess is it's top quality! His smile said it all, didn't it Vasilis?" asked Panos, who was the fourth member of this cheerful and fully energetic gathering.

"This weed is 'The Thing'. It's straight from Kalamata and it's super strong. It doesn't stop kicking in for hours and hours! We just need a two-paper joint for the four of us, especially after all this Ouzo. The old man who gave it to me is guaranty. And I'll make sure we have enough of it for our holidays in the islands." said Vasilis and raised his glass of Ouzo saying out loud "Yiamas boys!"

Between the four of them, they had drunk one and a half litre of Ouzo in the last hour. Four people who aren't regular drinkers, would have been sent to hell if they drank this quantity of Ouzo within one hour. Especially if it was consumed without any food, like these four did. But for them, it was another summer day, trying to achieve their goal of getting totally wasted by the end of the day.

"Let's finish our last glass and go to the stone slide at Saint John's woods, to hit this little beauty!" suggested Vasilis and continued: "Are you ok to drive your car Antonis? Or you want me to go and get it? I'll pick you all up from here. I'm not bothered to do that. I'm seriously energised right now my friend!"

"To be honest, if you brought the car, it would be spot on. I'm a bit pissed to drive, I think." answered Antonis, who was the only one in the group with a car.

"No worries. Just pass me the keys. I'll be back in no time." said Vasilis and left to pick up the car. He had already drunk too much alcohol to drive, but this didn't seem to be an issue for him. All he cared was to get stoned as soon as possible.

After a ten-minute walk, he reached the point where the car was parked. The first thing he did after he entered the car was to blast the speakers almost to the max with dance music.

Since he was in such a euphoric state, he thought his mates could wait for a few extra minutes. This way he could take a slightly longer route back to enjoy the moment all by himself.

While he was driving slowly around the town, with the windows down and the volume at twenty-eight out of thirty, he accidentally came across his younger brother Babis.

He was going back home after a visit to a friend's house. He was holding a monster-sandwich with the fillings overflowing out of it. His mouth was so full of food that his cheeks looked like two small balloons, ready to burst with the slightest touch.

"What the shit? Are you eating again? We had a full lunch three hours ago! What's wrong with you?" Vasilis challenged Babis after he stopped the car next to him, without lowering the volume of the music though.

"A. Ca. Hia. U." replied Babis as his mouth was ridiculously full of food.

"What? Say again!" Vasilis shouted back, as he couldn't understand what his brother was trying to tell him. He was quite drunk to realise that the music was too loud for two human beings to have a proper conversation, even if their mouths weren't ready to explode from the quantity of food stuck in them.

"A. Ca. Hia. U." Babis repeated. With his left hand, he pointed at his ear and made a movement indicating that he could hear shit. With his right hand, he was holding the monster-sandwich, from which the different types of sauces were slowly dripping towards his elbow. There was also a half-eaten tomato slice and a piece of boiled egg stuck on his chin.

"Ok, ok, I get it." said Vasilis and finally realised that he needs to turn the volume down to be able to communicate with his always-super-hungry brother. "Let's go again now. Are you a malaka? Are you eating again? We had a full lunch three hours ago. What's wrong with you?"

"I was hungry. What did you want me to do?" replied Babis after he swallowed quickly all the amount of food he had in his mouth, without even chewing it.

"Ooooohh! Screw this shit! I can't be asked right now. Come on, jump in the car. I'll drop you home quickly. I have some tunes to listen to, my little man! But clean yourself up first. I don't want you to spread shit all over the car with this stupid sandwich and your saucy hand. And remove this tomato and the egg from your chin. For God's sake!"

Babis just followed his brother's directions without any comment. He wiped his hand and mouth, wrapped the remaining of his monster-sandwich and got in the car.

"Nice one boy!" said Vasilis when Babis finally sat in the co-driver's sheet. He then gave him a friendly pat on his leg, showing him how happy he was having him there with him.

"Now listen to this tuuuune!" he exclaimed and the volume went back to twenty-eight out of thirty.

Babis seemed to enjoy the loud music and the whole scene.

He was moving his head to the rhythm and stretched his right hand outside the window. Vasilis was driving and dancing at the same time, which required a bit of a skill to achieve.

When they took the last turn just before their block of flats, a surprise was waiting for them around the corner.

A police car was parked almost seventy feet away in front of the church yard, and three cops were standing outside of it. Two of them, cop No2 and No3, were at the back, holding semi-automatic weapons. The third one, cop No1, who was standing a bit further at the front, was the one who raised his hand and signalled them to stop the car on the side.

To recap. A quick description of the status of the car and the passengers inside: none of them had a seat belt on, the electronic dance music was blasting out of the lowered windows and the driver had consumed a significant amount of Greek Ouzo, which contains 43–45% alcohol. Also, the driver had loose long hair, five piercings in both of his ears, nose and eyebrows, and a small bag of high-quality Kalamata weed in one of his pockets. And finally, the car didn't belong to him.

"We're done malaka! We're absolutely screwed now!!" Vasilis shouted horrified and continued: "How the fuck? All my life! I've never seen cops here! Never!"

As the cops were just a breath away, there wasn't enough time for Vasilis to make any major corrections, like putting the seat belts on, covering his Ouzo smelling breath and the most important of all, getting rid of the weed. What he was only able to correct was the music volume, which he turned down to zero. But Babis was also a factor of this complicated equation. Vasilis only had less than ten seconds to prepare him for what to expect and how to react.

"Listen to me very carefully! Don't worry at all. I'll deal with this. Relax and keep your mouth shut unless you're asked something directly. And do not contradict anything I say to the cops."

"Ok. But what's this 'contradict'?" asked Babis, who didn't seem to be particularly worrying. He wasn't aware of any critical points on which Vasilis was breaking the law and could find himself in good trouble.

"Screw it!!" shouted Vasilis as he didn't have the time to explain what 'contradict' means. "Just say to the cops that everything I say to them is totally true. Got it?"

"Ok. This is what I'll do then." answered Babis in a very reassuring manner.

When they stopped the car, cop No1 approached Vasilis' window. Cop No2 moved at the rear and No3 at the front of the car, both of them were still holding their semi-automatic guns, facing the ground.

"Driving Licence, Car Insurance and Car Taxation documents." said cop No1, who moved even closer to check the two passengers.

"Well, this car isn't mine. It belongs to my best friend. He's like a brother to me. But I'm not sure where the car documents are. I can quickly check in the glove box if that's ok with you. Unfortunately, I don't carry my Driving Licence with me, but my home is two minutes away and I can get it for you faster than you can imagine." Vasilis explained in such a persuasive manner that in any other circumstances, it could have worked. The main problem he had, apart from his wild look in the eyes of a Greek cop, with his long messy hair and five piercings, was the reeking smell of Ouzo coming out of his mouth. Whatever he would try to say or claim, he was already screwed, heading straight for an Alcohol Test.

"I can smell Ouzo here. Have you been drinking?" asked cop No1.

"I'm going to be honest with you Mister Police Officer. I drank a small shot of Ouzo a couple of minutes before I got into the car. It's my girlfriend's birthday today and I couldn't say no to her! You know how it goes with women! You always say yes to keep them happy! That's why it smells so much. I don't think this should be a problem." said Vasilis.

"You have a girlfriend? I didn't know that!" asked Babis full of surprise, but also very happy and proud for his big brother.

Vasilis turned his head and looked him in the eyes, with a look that could literally kill, and said: "She's a new one brother. I haven't told you anything about her yet."

Then he turned again to cop No1: "Babis is my little brother Mister Police Officer and I don't usually tell him all the details of my life." He then blinked his left eye to the cop.

Cop No1 wasn't quite persuaded and said: "Get out of the car slowly. Both of you. The driver will go through an Alcohol Test."

"I'm done now...

Properly done.

I'll break the breathalyser into parts...

If I blow in it after all this Ouzo...

Shit..." Vasilis' thought as he exited the car.

Babis on the other side, was still into his own world. He couldn't even imagine what all this meant and where it could lead to. He was only eleven years old and had absolutely no clue about the link between alcohol and driving.

"Stand over here. Place this into your mouth and blow in it with full power until you hear the beeping sound." said cop No1 as he held the breathalyser in front of Vasilis' mouth.

Vasilis followed the instructions given to the letter. He was aware that the percentage of alcohol in the exhaled air would determine the level of how deeply screwed he was, but he wasn't exactly sure about the fines linked to different alcohol levels. No need to bring up Babis' expertise on the matter; it was all a blur in the darkness of uncertainty.

After a couple of seconds, the breathalyser had the result.

When cop No1 saw the reading, his head made a sudden reflective movement forward and his eyes went wide-open, as if he couldn't believe what he was actually seeing. Cop No2 and No3 made a step forward and raised their semi-automatic weapons slightly, after they saw the reaction of their colleague.

"You have a serious problem. The result is 1.53mg/lt. Do you have any idea what this means for you?" cop No1 asked Vasilis.

"Not exactly to be honest, but I can assure you Mr Police Officer that I'm feeling completely fine and sober to drive home and drop my little brother off, who's not so little as you can see by the way!" said Vasilis and laughed nervously. He hoped that his attempt at humour would tickle the cops' funny bone and lead to an easy escape, relying on his impressive comedy talents.

No cop laughed.

"I'll break this down to you as simply as possible. There're different levels of penalties based on the alcohol readings from this machine. The highest level of penalty is when the reading is over 1.10mg/lt." said cop No1 and before he managed to complete what he was trying to explain, Babis looked at Vasilis and asked him out-loud: "So this makes you a winner Vasilis??"

All three cops burst into laughter, not just at the question's absurdity but also at how it was delivered with impeccable timing.

"It's not a video-game malaka! Shut your mouth and don't speak again. Do you understand?" Vasilis whispered to Babis when all the cops were still laughing and he nodded back in agreement.

When the cops' laughing session came to an end, cop No1 continued: "A reading over 1.10mg/lt means immediate arrest and court action. This can result in losing your driving licence for one year minimum, imprisonment for one month minimum and a five hundred thousand Greek Drachmas minimum fine. And since it's late Friday and the courts are closed for the weekend, you'll have to be arrested and spend three nights in custody until Monday morning, when the courts are open again. This is only for the alcohol part of the story. You also had no seat belts on, didn't carry your driving licence, didn't show us any documents for the car and there's still a body search we need to complete at the police station. This may change the course of things. You never know what we can find in the weirdest of places. Trust me."

"Vasilis, I need to pee!!" shouted Babis. This was one of his usual reactions when he was getting overly stressed.

"Shut up!" Vasilis shouted angrily back at him and then turned to cop No1.

He put in action his most miserable and pathetic manner and started with the begging: "Mister Police Officer... With all the respect... Please don't make this such a big deal, I'm begging you! I've been having serious family problems in the last year and this makes me drink sometimes. I'm really sorry and embarrassed that I lied to you, but I was completely scared to tell you the truth. And this is because of my abusive father. He is beating me and our mummy (he never called Soula mummy in real life). The beatings are so severe that all the neighbours can hear us. This happens every day when he returns home drunk. And he must have beaten our mummy again because I met one of our neighbours when I was leaving my girlfriend's place and told me that he could hear loads of shouting and banging from our flat. And I'm so scared for my mummy now! That's why I drove the car straight after I drank a tiny bit of Ouzo with my girlfriend. I only wanted to go and save my mummy from this monster!"

"Oh my God!! When did all these happen? Why didn't you say anything to me?" Babis screamed out of nowhere and started crying.

"Come over here little one. Don't worry. We'll help you and your mummy. Now please stop crying." said cop No1 to Babis and gave him kind of a hug.

"Thank you..." replied Babis and almost stopped crying.

"Do you live in the same house with him?" cop No1 asked Babis.

"Yes. He's my brother." answered Babis.

"Have you heard your mother screaming when you're home at any time?" cop No1 asked him again.

"Yes. I have. She screams at my dad that he's 'useless' and 'lazy' and he's 'like a child' all the time." answered Babis.

"And what your dad does after?" asked cop No1.

"He asks her to forgive him and he says he'll never do it again. And sometimes he's crying alone locked in the bathroom and I heard him again yesterday."

At that point, Vasilis came into the bitter realisation that his brother had screwed him gigantically.

"Right. I'll tell you how it goes for you now. Because you found me in a good mood today and I'm also amused by your little brother, who I like because he's honest and innocent, the exact opposite of what you are, I'll give you one more final chance. In ten minutes, you'll blow the breathalyser again. I'll let you go grab a chocolate and a bottle of water from this kiosk over there. If the reading doesn't fall under 1.10mg/lt, you're coming with us and stay in custody until Monday morning, when you'll go to court. If you even think about giving your little brother a hostile look or laying a finger on him, you're going to regret it, big time. You'll have to do with me. Got it?" said cop No1 to Vasilis, who was looking down to the ground like a five-year-old boy, caught red-handed eating chocolate from the forbidden cupboard.

Vasilis had no other choice than to take the cop's offer, which could actually be a blessing in disguise. The little kiosk was on the other side of the road, roughly about sixty feet away from them. Unexpectedly, the cops stayed in their positions and let him walk there, to get a chocolate and a bottle of water, all by himself. They occupied themselves by bombarding Babis with questions and then bursting into laughter at his responses and the amusing way he engaged with them.

This offered him an unbelievable opportunity to get rid of the weed, which was still waiting patiently in his front pocket. When he reached the fridge to get the bottle of water, he pretended that the chocolate bar fell off his hands and bent on his knees to pick it up. A counter in front of the fridge was creating a blind spot between him and the cops when he was down to the ground. Within milliseconds, he put his right hand inside his pocket, picked the little bag, pushed it under the fridge and stood up again. At least, he was weed-free now.

"Ok. You know the drill. Stand over here again. Place this into your mouth and blow." said cop No1 after Vasilis had eaten a big chocolate bar and drunk a 500ml bottle of water.

The beeping sound was heard.

Vasilis closed his eyes and waited for the verdict.

"It's unbelievable!" exclaimed cop No1.

Vasilis opened his eyes full of hope that the reading was lower than 1.10mg/lt at last.

"It's 1.56mg/lt! Instead of going down, it went up! I can't remember seeing anything like this before!" said cop No1 fully surprised.

After this, without any further discussion, Vasilis would be taken by the cops to the local police station. As cop No1 had already made very clear to him, he would spend the following three nights in a cell, until he was taken to court in front of a judge on Monday morning.

Before he entered the police car in handcuffs, the cops allowed him to make two quick phone calls. He firstly called his mate Antonis and explained what had happened. He also told him that he had left the car keys with Babis, who would wait for him at the point where the cops stopped them. He then called his mother Soula to inform her about his 'bad luck' and what might happen to him.

The time he entered the little cell in the police station, where he would spend the three following nights, was 7:55pm on Friday evening. At 9:32pm, a cop approached his cell and said: "Get up. You're clear to go. Your case is closed."

"What?... I mean... How??..." Vasilis couldn't process what he just heard. "I don't understand!"

"Me too, to be honest. We just follow orders here. You must have some very powerful friends. There's no way on earth for someone with a case like yours, to walk free in less than two hours..." said the cop as she unlocked his cell.

Behind the scenes; Soula felt completely helpless when Vasilis called her. She thought that only one person could support them in this case and this was Lupo. Therefore, she called him straight away and asked for his help. It only took him a couple of phone calls to have Vasilis cleared and released in less than two hours. Even if it was Friday evening and everything was already closed for the weekend...

The first thing Vasilis did after he was released was to call Antonis to pick him up from the police station. Then, they drove to the kiosk where he had hidden the weed. The little bag was still there waiting for him under the fridge and he felt so emotional to hold it in his hands again.

Following this touching moment, they picked up the other two, Louis and Panos, and headed to Saint John's woods. That night, they blazed through the entire bag at the stone slide.

8:50pm, Thursday 13th May 2010

"Grab Soula with Babis and I'll go ahead to keep the route clear. Tell me when ready." Vasilis asked Lupo and moved towards the door which led to the back storage room. Both Lupo and Babis followed his lead and managed to move Soula with surgical accuracy at the back storage room, where they successfully placed her on the bed there.

On the other side of this relatively big room, sixteen-year-old Fotis, the second assistant to the assistant waiters, was trying to get some extra napkins as they were running low in the taverna. When Babis realised this, he asked him to get out of there at once, to avoid seeing the rest. However, he committed a critical error. He forgot to make it crystal clear to Fotis that, no matter who asked him, he mustn't say that Babis was at the back storage room.

After a few seconds and some water splashed on her face, Soula regained consciousness. This allowed Lupo to begin.

"Just before 8pm today, a good friend from the neighbourhood gave me a call about something you'll have to help me with. This good friend was at the park, walking his dog around the lake. He told me that even though he was at a distance and it was getting dark, he saw Barbara walking from the back of a kiosk and then towards the exit of the park. This made him suspicious and moved towards the kiosk. Then a man appeared from the back of the kiosk and walked fast to the opposite direction to Barbara. He couldn't tell who that man was, so he decided to follow him. That man, after he left the park, came straight into your taverna. My good friend is certain it was Tasos." said Lupo at a very steady pace, without raising his voice at any point, which creeped everyone out.

"So. Where is Tasos?" asked Lupo in a don't-even-think-of-giving-me-any-bullshit-now tone.

Babis and Soula's hearts stopped and their breath caught in their throats. They were both frozen in place and looked too terrified to even move.

"Tasos isn't here Nikolas. None of us saw him tonight. Are you sure your friend is right?" answered Vasilis trying to stall for some time, until he came up with a solution to this Gordian knot. He was certain that if Lupo came across Tasos, he would seriously harm him.

"Vasilis listen to me very carefully. This is the final time I'm asking before I go around and search every inch of this fuckin taverna. And I won't stop until I find the little bastard. Where. The fuck. Is. Tasos." said Lupo in the most don't-even-think-of-giving-me-any-bullshit-now-or-there-will-be-blood tone possible.

And just when Lupo finished his sentence, the storage room door opened and a man shouted: "Babis! Are you here? I couldn't wait in that toilet any longer."

It was Tasos.

After Babis left him in the toilet to sort out the issue with Soula, Tasos' patience ended, and he popped out of there. The first person he came across was the sixteen-year-old Fotis, the second assistant to the assistant waiters. He asked him if he had seen Babis and Fotis told him that he was at the back storage room. And this is exactly where he went without a second thought.

Tasos' voice cut through the air like a knife, making everyone pause with immediate effect. Soula fainted for one more time before she even managed to say another word. But nobody seemed to care about it. His arrival was hotter than anything else.

Tasos walked towards the back of the room, where he came across Babis, Vasilis and Soula lying motionless on the bed (Round II). The last thing he saw was Lupo's figure standing in front of him, which made him shit himself. Literally. Experiencing sheer horror, his rear end reacted by dropping a small, solid piece.

What do they want from us?

Various organized crime elements originating from Greece were commonly referred to as the 'Greek Mafia'. Indigenous criminal groups had firmly established themselves in the largest Greek urban centres, particularly in Athens. However, it is important to note that large-scale organized crime, such as the Greek Mafia, should not be confused with Greek street gangs, who engaged in smaller street crimes.

Apart from domestic criminal organisations, the Sicilian Mafia, Camorra, Albanian, Romanian and Serbian mafia groups had also been operating in Greece in collaboration with the domestic criminal syndicates. Locally, Greek crime bosses were commonly referred to as 'Godfathers of the night'. They mainly operated as owners of nightclubs and other entertainment businesses, using these locations as bases for organising their illegal activities and money laundering.

Lupo, over the years and having started his career in crime from the age of fourteen, had managed to become one of the strongest 'Godfathers of the night'. His base of operations was in Athens, the Greek capital with a population exceeding four million people.

Big part of his organisation's success was based on 'dirty' politicians in every government and corrupt officials in various public services. The main public service he had the best cooperation throughout the years was the Greek Police Force. Every given time, he had in his payroll top level cops who offered him protection and valuable information.

Lupo had always in his mind one phrase his grandad used to say a lot: *'filaye ta ruha su, na ehis ta misa'. (φύλαγε τα ρούχα σου, να έχεις τα μισά). [literal translation: take guard of your clothes, so you can have half of them. This phrase praises the act of being careful and proactive to minimize potential future losses.]*

For every single interaction and transaction he made with all the different politicians, cops and other officials, he always kept records. These included videos and voice recordings, photos and screenshots of dialogues. With these pieces of evidence, he blackmailed them to keep quiet, obedient and continue 'working' for him, as he was holding them firmly by their balls.

This enabled his organisation to be very efficient and productive, but mainly highly motivated to achieve their business targets. Their specialisation was in activities such as racketeering and selling 'protection services' to other businesses, money laundering and weapon & drug trafficking.

Lupo, apart from the three nightclubs he owned, he had also built a number of other legitimate businesses. The primary ones included a substantial construction company, specialising in both private and public projects, a real estate brand and a waste management company. Through all these, he was able to launder all the dirty money coming from his very busy and successful underground businesses. As a result, he had accumulated a big amount of wealth, with his estimated net worth reaching over 200 million euros in 2008. All this money was in several offshore accounts and shell businesses, making it pretty much untraceable.

However, being in this trade comes with plenty of problems. Lupo didn't like problems, he was severely allergic to them. So, when there was one, he made sure it went away one way or another, before he got an anaphylactic shock from it. If it was a stubborn one like a huge painful nasty haemorrhoid, he was forced to implement the most extreme solution of all...

"Have a seat." said Lupo when Kostas, his right hand and number two in the rank of his organisation, walked into his office in one of his nightclubs. Lupo was smoking a big cigar and there was whisky in his glass. No ice, no water, just whisky. Straight.

It was 2:45pm on Friday 11th April 2008. The club was empty, just the men from Lupo's personal security were scattered in different posts inside, but also outside of it.

"What did they say?" asked Kostas and lit up a cigarette.

"It's all fucked. It doesn't look good." answered Lupo and drank all the remaining whisky in his glass with one sip.

Kostas didn't ask anything else. He knew Lupo would explain more to him.

"They're angry. Very angry." said Lupo and stopped to take a puff from his long Cuban cigar. Then, he left it on the ashtray and looked at Kostas in the eyes. He banged the office with his right hand and shouted: "I'm pissed off too! Very fuckin pissed off!"

He stood up from his chair. He walked and talked at the same time around the room. "That little cocksucker Andreas *(the Greek Minister of Justice)* told me that he'll be out if he didn't solve the problem until the end of next week. Then, the other malaka Manolis *(the Chief of the Greek Police)*, told me that he received the exact same warning."

He stopped walking and took a good puff from his big cigar.

"These sons of bitches believe that they can threaten me... *Tha mu klasune ta arhithia! (θα μου κλάσουνε τα αρχίδια!) [literal translation: they will fart on my testicles. This very popular cocky Greek phrase is used to demonstrate superiority and dominance against your opponent who are supposedly not strong enough to cause any damage to you, even to the slightest extent.]*

He then approached Kostas, who was still sitting on his chair in front of the office, bent over him and screamed at his face: "Fuck them all! Fuck them! I fuckin hate their guts! All of them! The scumbags!"

"What do they want from us?" asked Kostas calmly.

"To solve the problem. By next Friday. That's what they want." replied Lupo abruptly and took another puff from his Cuban cigar.

"I think that's the only way. This fucker didn't seem to care about anything we have tried so far. All our threats did fuck-all to him. We even sent the tax-men to threaten him and his boss to shut them down and send them to slammer, but nothing. He kept writing and writing and fuckin writing... And he keeps going to the live news to make his fuckin revelations. What a malaka is this? I think he's crazy in the fuckin head. I don't think we have any other option..." said Kostas.

"I know, I know." Lupo agreed with his associate and sat back down at his black-leather office chair.

He refilled his glass with whisky and took a good sip down. Then he took another big puff from his cigar. He looked at Kostas and said: "Ok. Albanian twins it is."

A week after, on Friday 18th April 2008, the following article was published in one the biggest news websites in Greece:

"With a laser-like focus, Antonopoulos' articles pierced the darkness surrounding the intricate web of connections between powerful players on all "four sides": police, organized crime, businesspeople and politicians. His words shone a light on the unsettling reality of high-ranking police officials dabbling in the illicit world of organized crime, acting as personal security for dangerous mafia bosses, while keeping a delicate balance of power between various interests. Antonopoulos didn't shy away from exposing the corrupt actions of National Intelligence Service agents, who engaged in illegal phone tracking and even plotted murders to shield the mafia's interests, while discrediting honest officers in the process.

The forensic analysis was alarming. Out of the sixteen bullets discharged at the prominent journalist, only two missed their mark and hit his car instead. From the remaining shots, three struck him on his left arm, one on his neck, seven on his chest and three on his head. The latter three were the fatal blows, leading to instantaneous death.

The ballistics investigation revealed that the automatic rifle used by the perpetrators was "clean", meaning it had not been previously used before that April 17th afternoon. At noon, the police editor was returning home to Glyfada after appearing on the prime time TV news. Four construction workers who were present at the time recounted their experience, stating that they heard a sound resembling an exhaust, followed by additional noises. When they turned around, they saw the journalist fall to the ground.

The entire event lasted no longer than twenty seconds. The executioners did not speak or communicate in any way and they swiftly departed the crime scene on their sport-bike.

The perpetrators were familiar with Grigoris Antonopoulos' routine and knew the exact time he returned home every day. The police are investigating the possibility that additional individuals provided support and monitored the situation. None of the witnesses were able to identify the perpetrators or provide any useful information. 'There was no sign of them. The image that remains with me is of the man in the military jacket executing.' one of the construction workers said, adding that the sound of the automatic rifle was similar to that of an exhaust. However, he did not have enough time to take note of the license plate of their sport-bike.

Since the incident, the question remains unanswered: who wanted the journalist dead? The police are examining various scenarios, but all agree that the journalist may have upset the local mafia with his occasional revelations. Initial reports indicate that he did not disclose any threats to his colleagues or request police protection."

8:56pm, Thursday 13th May 2010

*"Kalos ta arhithia mas ta thio! (Καλώς τα αρχίδια μας τα δυό)
[literal translation: Welcome our testicles the two. This cheerful
phrase, often considered the epitome of the Greek hospitality,
is used when you want to patronise the arrival of a person
who is not liked or welcomed.]* We've been waiting for you!
Ooohh! Don't be like that now! Come closer and join our little
party!" said Lupo dripping with sarcasm, when he saw Tasos
standing frozen like an ancient Greek statue.

"So. Vasilis and little Babis of course. You didn't know where
Tasos was, eh?" asked Lupo staring into Vasilis eyes.

"Let me explain..." Vasilis tried to answer as Babis, in the
best-case scenario, would recover his ability to speak the
next day, provided he was still among the living.

Lupo cut him off. He walked towards them and repeated
his question. "So. Vasilis and little Babis of course. None of
you had seen Tasos tonight, eh? Does it say 'malaka' on my
forehead, you little bastards? Does it?"

He then moved like a thunder and slapped Vasilis on the face
in such a forceful way, he almost sent him to the ground.
Babis' brotherly instinct made him push Lupo with all his
power, which sent him almost flying and landing on the
sacks of onions and potatoes.

That was it. The fight had officially begun.

Lupo was a street fighter, a beast of a man with a heavy build
and a mean streak. He was hard to manage in a fight and even
harder to beat. But now he was facing three strong young
men, all fighting for their own survival. This wasn't going to
be a walk in the park for any of them.

When Lupo rose from the sack of onions and potatoes,
he punched Vasilis on the face, sending him away with a
bleeding nose. He then moved towards Tasos, his main target
for the day. Tasos tried to avoid him with a dance move; he

pretended to move to his right and then moved to his left, but Lupo wasn't tricked. He managed to grab him by the throat and shouted: "Did you fuck Barbara, you cunt? I 'll kill you fucker!"

Now, only Babis was available to save Tasos. To fight Lupo alone, he had to rely on his main weapon: his grip, which was similar to that of a one-hundred-and-twenty-stone grizzly bear. If someone tried to escape from it, Babis would just squeeze tighter, forcing his victim to either surrender or lose consciousness.

And that's what he exactly did.

He grabbed Lupo from the back and immobilised him by squeezing him with all the power he had inside him. His target was to compel Lupo to release Tasos, whose face had shifted to a purple tone. Despite that bear grab, Lupo wouldn't let Tasos' throat free and it was a matter of seconds before he was choked to death.

"Let him go now or I crash your head motherfucker!" Vasilis screamed with his face full of blood and moved fast towards Lupo. His right hand was raised in the air holding a big hammer, ready to land it on Lupo's head.

"No Vasilis! No! Don't do it! He's your father! Stop Vasilis! Nikolas is your real father!!" screamed Soula, who regained her consciousness from Vasilis' scream just before he hit Lupo's head with the hammer.

Everyone froze immediately.

Four seconds of deafening silence followed.

....

"I'm gay and me and Lakis love each other!!" Babis' loud announcement to everyone in the room, broke the deadly silence.

Deciding to say the wrong thing at the worst time possible, was one of the side effects from the overwhelming pressure he was under. Another side effect was the delay his brain experienced in sending the correct signals to his body parts.

He was still holding Lupo like a grizzly bear, when he made the official announcement to everyone in the room.

"Shut up malaka Babis! Just shut the fuck up now, you idiot!" Vasilis exploded at him, not having processed what his little brother had just announced.

He then turned his head towards his mother and with an almost dying voice, he barely managed to complete the following question: "What did you just say Soula??..."

He dropped the hammer on the floor and moved towards her direction. His steps were slow and unsteady. He was looking for a place to sit. This revelation by his own mother hit him like thunder striking a lonely tree on a mountain.

God forgive me for this sin

"I can't believe it! I honestly can't! I'm really, really, reeeeaaaally exhausted from all this. I don't know what to say... I don't know what to feel any more... And I don't know what else I can do... I just want to give up. That's it! I'm done with it! Kaput!" Soula declared to Ilias.

"Come on now Soula! Don't be like this... We can't stop trying! You know hope dies last, don't you?" Ilias pleaded with her to reconsider her decision to abort the efforts they were both making for a while now.

"Don't talk to me about hope! Please don't! Because you're making things worse than they actually are." responded Soula abruptly. "I'm the only one who's been running from church to church. I'm the only one speaking with all the priests to get their blessing. I'm the only one who's been running like a lunatic from monastery to monastery to pray with the monks and the nuns. So! Please! Don't talk to me about hope! Ok?"

"Wait a minute. What are you saying? That I don't care about it at all? That's what you think? Are you for real?" asked Ilias who was also getting worked up like Soula.

"To be honest, you could do with a bit of extra effort in specific areas, don't you think? When you come to me to have sex with your breath smelling of tzatziki, wearing your stupid-white-only-grandpas-wear-this-shitty-full-of-holes underwear that you don't let me bin by the way, and then you're always in a rush to finish with me quickly like I'm a whore for whom you have no loving feelings, no, I don't think you honestly care!" Soula lashed out at him and continued: "What do you think I am? A plastic doll with no heart and brain? Listen to me now carefully Ilias. There's no way I'll ever get pregnant from you if you don't change all the things I just said. Not some of them. All of them! Do you understand me? Because if you don't, you won't ever be able to lay an eye between my legs again until you die! And I mean it!"

"Nobody speaks to me like this! Do you understand stupid woman?" Ilias snapped at her after all the 'offensive' comments he received.

But he didn't stop there. As he went ballistic, he raised his right hand and was ready to hit her.

"If you dare to even touch me, I am gone!! Forever!!" Soula screamed back so loudly that she scared Ilias, making him to pull his hand back down and walk away.

The tension between them had been building for quite a while and on that day, it reached a breaking point. They couldn't help themselves but to clash in a serious way. They had been trying to have a baby almost since they got married, but they weren't successful and one more negative result from a pregnancy test derailed them.

Even though Soula was extremely religious, she was very open-minded about the pregnancy issue they were facing. She had even suggested to Ilias that she was willing to travel to England to take part in the In Vitro Fertilisation (IVF) procedure, which was a historic scientific breakthrough in that period. She had heard that the year before, in 1978, the first successful IVF pregnancy and live birth had occurred by two doctors who had performed the procedure in Manchester, UK.

She was convinced that this was their only option after all the unsuccessful attempts they had experienced up to that point. She was prepared to go to any lengths to have a family with him, regardless of the emotional or physical toll this might take on her.

But Ilias was a classic Greek malaka. An old-school male, full of sick ego and unjustified pride of himself. He could be as stubborn as a mule no matter if he was in the wrong. And most of all, he would rather die than let any neighbour, relative or friend, gossip about him being incapable of getting his wife pregnant.

He genuinely believed that he was a *'magas' (μάγκας)*. *[This Greek term is used for a person who is characterized by excessive self-confidence or arrogance, as well as a distinctive appearance or behaviour that is different from the norm. A type of an ordinary man who pretends to be a tough guy and who often makes a show of his strength. 90% of the Greek male population belonged to this category. There was a magas almost in every Greek man.]*

Therefore, as a big magas he pretended to be, he wouldn't even agree to have a fertility test. He had also convinced Soula, or so he thought, that it was only up to God whether she would ever get pregnant or not. So, Soula being religious to the bone, had turned to God for help as she couldn't use any scientific help due to the overwhelming Greek pride and sense of manhood from this magas.

But God seemed unwilling to get her pregnant as well. He had done this once with a Mary a long time ago and it had caused kind of a chaotic environment afterwards. Therefore, God must have decided to avoid that scenario, to prevent a potential mayhem in round II.

After Ilias walked away from her, he went to their bedroom and changed his clothes. He then left the flat with a big bang behind him when he closed the main door. He didn't say a word to her.

This was something he used to do a lot during the last period, whenever there was a heated argument between them. He would leave Soula alone and go to a coffee-bar in the city centre. This was the meeting point with his mates, who each one of them was also a *'magas'* like him.

This coffee-bar was full of men drinking coffee, alcohol, watching sports, mainly football, playing cards and smoking.

Heavily smoking.

They were smoking so much that in the wintertime, due to the cold and moist atmosphere outside, when someone opened the main door, the cloud of smoke that billowed out was thick enough to make you call the fire service. And the smell was something else in there. It was a mixture of smoke from cigarettes, cigars & pipes, Greek Ouzo, Greek coffee and Greek manhood in the form of armpit sweat and grimy body odours.

But the biggest attraction of this place was its toilets. The owners didn't even bother to divide them between men and women. This would be completely pointless as there were always only men in their coffee-bar. The staff working in there was only men as well. This had resulted in such filthy and mucky toilets, with a distinctive foul smell of urine, so strong that could make your eyes cry. These toilets could easily win the 'Worst Toilet in Greece' award.

Ilias had been drinking a lot in the last two months. Most of the time, he returned home in the early hours of the day, as drunk as a skunk. The time he banged the door behind him and disappeared was 7:35pm, on Tuesday 6th November 1979.

After the loud bang on the door, Soula burst into tears and cried for over an hour, lying on their bed.

She was so depressed by the turn her life had taken. She always dreamed of starting a family, but not getting pregnant had become a constant source of pain and disappointment. She knew very well that Ilias wanted a child as well. Therefore, she couldn't help feeling that she was also letting him down in her own way. The initial connection they had once shared was fading and her feelings for him were becoming increasingly negative every day. Being left home alone night after night, when he was getting drunk with his 'friends' at that repulsive coffee-bar, also played a big part in this.

At the same time, her heart ached as she thought about her old friends. It had been so long since she had seen them and missed their company terribly. She missed the pure laughter, the stories they shared and their sense of belonging to each other. She felt like she was drifting far away from them and didn't really know how to reconnect. But the thing that had affected her the most was the feeling her sex life was worse than a prostitute's...

 When she had no more tears left to shed, she rose from the bed feeling drained and hopeless. She thought that a walk outside in the cold, fresh air might help clear her head and refresh her mood.

But, after crying for over an hour, the mirror didn't do any favour to her when she looked at it, just before she was about to leave the flat. Her face was a mess with her eyes red and swollen, but she didn't care at all about it. All she wanted was to get out of there as soon as possible. Without a second thought, she put on a jacket, wore the first pair of shoes she found in front of her and left the flat as if she was chased by a serial killer.

Given her mental and physical state, the ideal scenario in her mind was to move like a quick shadow. She wanted to be unseen, unheard and unnoticed by any neighbour, until she reached the local park. There, it would be clear of any people at that time, as it was already dark outside.

This didn't go as planned. She didn't even make it three steps out of the main entrance of their block of flats before she came across Lupo.

Soula knew Lupo for many years as they were living in the same neighbourhood. They would always have catch ups whenever they met. She knew very well that he had his dark side and was part of the Mafia. But she never actually minded about his activities, as long as she and Ilias and were not directly affected by them.

"Hello Soula. How're you my dear?" asked Lupo in a very pleasant manner, expressing that he was genuinely very delighted to meet her.

"Hi. I'm ok." she replied with an almost dead voice, without making any direct eye contact and looking down to the ground.

"What's wrong Soula?" he asked back as it was obvious to him that something wasn't right with her.

"Nothing. Honestly, nothing." she replied with the same weak tone, still looking down to the ground, avoiding any direct eye contact with him.

Lupo decided to take action. He moved a step closer to her, placed his right hand gently on her left shoulder and asked her calmly: "Who hurt you Soula?"

These four words were enough for her to break into tears. She couldn't hold it any longer.

Lupo wasn't expecting this to happen so suddenly, but he acted very swiftly. He hugged her with both of his hands and let her cry literally on his shoulder. He avoided saying anything to her while she was breathing heavily and sobbing. He waited patiently until she calmed down and could have a conversation again.

But he faced a serious technical problem. While he hugged her, their bodies came so close to each other. Her massive breasts were squeezed on him and he ended up having a proper boner.

"*For fuck's shake...*

It's not the right time to get a stiffy...

Shit!" he initially thought while he was getting harder and harder.

Not many seconds later, his thoughts took a U turn.

"*Now that I'm thinking about it, I would definitely do her!*

She mustn't have had it properly for a long time.

Ilias is a useless malaka anyway.

Never liked this prick...

If she's up for it, I'll give her the best one she had in her life..."

"Let's go back inside Soula. I don't want anyone from the neighbourhood to see us here." he whispered in her ear, after the first strong wave of crying had passed.

This way they would avoid being seen in this state by all the nosy neighbours, who would make things completely worse with their interference and commentary. Most of them were living to gossip and the rest were gossiping to live. Moving quickly back inside the block of flats was a no brainer.

"Thank you so much for looking after me Nikolas..." said Soula who was still crying, but at a lower intensity now.

"Listen Soula. I don't know where you were planning to go, but it's not the best idea to be out there on your own now. Before I met you, in just two minutes, I spoke to three different groups of people who all know you. If they see you, they'll grill you. You can't deal with them right now." Lupo explained to her calmly by holding both of her shoulders and looking straight into her eyes.

"I wanted to go to the park to clear my head... But now I'm scared of all these 'black hawks out there waiting for their prey'." said Soula after she considered carefully what Lupo explained to her.

Then she continued: "I'm not feeling very well Nikolas... I feel I'll explode... I'm at a breaking point... I need to speak to someone... I really need to speak to someone who'll listen to me..."

She started crying again and begged him: "Can you please come upstairs for a bit? Please Nikolas... I need to take some things out of my chest. Ilias has left and won't be back until late tonight or tomorrow. I don't even know anymore..."

"Come with me Soula. Let's go upstairs." said Lupo. He put his arm around her and helped her to walk towards the elevator. He was rock hard now.

On the other side, Soula's emotions were deeply conflicted due to Ilias' neglect and mistreatment. She was constantly feeling unloved and undervalued in her marriage, which weighed heavily on her self-esteem. So, she felt that Lupo genuinely cared for her well-being, which resulted in a profound sense of relief and happiness washing over her. His kindness and thoughtful gestures, since she met him downstairs, made her feel special and cherished. His strong and masculine presence made her experience a newfound sense of self-worth and femininity. The small chunk of warmth and care he offered her, begun to fast-heal the emotional wounds inflicted by Ilias, allowing her to embrace once again her own worth and feel like a loved and valued woman.

When the elevator reached the third floor, they got out of it very quickly. They went straight into her flat, moving at maximum speed to avoid being seen by any neighbours. When they were finally inside and closed the door behind them, Soula, without even thinking, hugged him with all her heart again.

That was enough for Lupo. He pulled her face towards his and kissed her. Soula didn't oppose to it. They continued kissing deeply and passionately. They were both so lustful that things escalated very quickly as their adrenaline was hitting highs. They didn't even try to go to the bedroom.

Soula turned her head towards the ceiling, made the sign of the cross on her and said: "God forgive me for this sin..." Then she turned her back to Lupo and asked him in a seductive but also demanding tone: "Make love to me now!"

Lupo put his mouth next to her ear and with a low and hot voice, he whispered: "I want you badly Soula! You're so beautiful! I'm crazy for you!"

They started slowly, but it didn't take long until they were pounding on each other. After two whole minutes, mainly with Soula shouting to God out of pleasure and seeking for His forgiveness simultaneously, this 'sex of a lifetime' was coming to an end.

"Oh God! Oooooh God! Jesus Christ and virgin Mary!!!" shouted Soula, just enough so she couldn't be heard by her nosy neighbours.

"I'm cumming! I'm cumming!" moaned Lupo in such a good synchrony with her. This is when she grabbed him with all her power from both of his butt-cheeks and didn't let him go until he finished ejaculating inside her up to the last drop.

Lupo didn't seem to care to the slightest degree about it and what might follow.

But Soula did.

This 'sex of a lifetime' and the way it was concluded, could change everything about her future. It could put an end to all the drama with Ilias and the failed attempts to have a baby during the last period.

And it did.

Little Vasilis was born nine months later.

8:59pm, Thursday 13th May 2010

Soula's mind-blowing revelation shook everyone in the storage room and brought the brawl to an end. Lupo, who had just saved his skull from Vasilis' hammer hit, released Tasos' throat just before he passed out. But Babis was still a few paces behind. He continued holding Lupo tightly and only released him after his future father-in-law shouted back at him: "You can let me go now genious!"

When Lupo was released, he turned around and said sarcastically to Babis: "You almost gave me a stiffy with your tits, malaka." His pyramid tits were squeezing Lupo's back quite hard all the time he was bear-grabbed.

Vasilis staggered to the bed where Soula was sitting. He slumped down next to her, with his body as limp as a rag doll. He was utterly stunned by what he had just heard from her.

"Explain what you just said Soula…" Vasilis asked her.

Soula had no choice but to finally reveal the hidden truth she had been keeping from everyone for all these years. Only Lupo knew about it and she could no longer keep it bottled up inside.

"My sweet boy… I need you to understand me… Please don't judge me. What has happened cannot change. We can only look ahead now…" Soula said, trying to ease into what she was about to reveal.

Vasilis didn't respond at all. He just listened while staring at her.

"We were trying to have our first baby with your father for long time, but we couldn't. And we were pushing it too much. We had tried everything. Doctors, prayers, visits to monasteries. Everything we could. But nothing. It was tearing us apart and we were fighting almost every day. I was so depressed with my life. I was feeling that even God had forgotten about me. I was even thinking to get a divorce. I

160

couldn't stand it any longer... One day, when I was in a very bad state, I came across Nikolas. He helped me so much that day. I was so desperate and Nikolas was there for me. God had listened to my prayers and send him to me that day..."

Soula stopped talking. Her eyes dropped to the floor and her face was burning with shame. She couldn't bring herself to look back at Vasilis.

"And??" asked Vasilis loudly.

"And that was the day I got pregnant with you. That's it. I said it! I said it! Jesus Christ, forgive me for my sins..." Soula looked with her eyes wide open at the ceiling and made the sign of the cross on her. She then took a deep breath followed by a massive exhale and continued: "After a month, when I said to your father that I was pregnant, he was over the moon. I wouldn't spoil his joy for any reason in the world. And I never did. Ilias, until he died, always believed that you're his son..."

"I knew it!" shouted Babis like he made the discovery of the century. "I knew it! How didn't you see this all this time? Look how shorter he is than me! And look at the colour of his hair too! Just look! All of you! Look!"

Nobody responded.

It all made more sense in Vasilis' head now. Lupo had been helping him and Soula one way or another for years, especially after his father dropped dead from his Ecstasy pills. Every time they asked him for anything, he was always there for them.

Soula on the other side... He thought that she shared everything with him. How could she keep this secret for so many years? He just couldn't believe it. His whole world was reset in just a few seconds...

But he didn't have the time he needed to reflect on all these. There was a hot-button issue demanding urgent resolution: how to keep Tasos alive and what Lupo would demand to guarantee this.

"Come with me Vasilis. We need to speak. Just you and me. The rest of you don't move. Wait here until we're back.

Especially you Tasos. Don't you even think about getting out of this fuckin room." said Lupo and walked towards the door of the storage room. Vasilis followed him.

Lupo was walking three steps in front of Vasilis all the time, until he reached his car, which was parked close to the taverna.

"Get inside." he ordered Vasilis.

When they were both in the car, Vasilis was lost for words. His mind was racing, trying to process everything that had happened in the last twenty minutes. It was all too much to take in. He was staring out the windscreen without saying a word.

"I know how hard it is for you now." said Lupo.

Vasilis didn't respond. He didn't even turn his head, continuing to stare outside the car.

"I want you to know that I care for you and Soula. She's a good woman. She has been through a lot. I did my best all these years to help her whenever I could. And you know this. I watched you growing up from a little boy to the man you're now. I'm so proud of you. I could even see myself in you. And I kept you out of big trouble when you messed things up. The cops knew all the time about you pushing drugs. But I ordered them to stay put."

Vasilis was gobsmacked on how to react.

"Why didn't you say you're my real father all these years?

You bastard!

Why the hell??

But you had always been there for me and Soula.

Every time we needed your help.

Every single time.

You were always there.

You even saved my ass from the cops.

I know...

How can I challenge you?

How can I challenge a godfather of the night like you?

What will happen to me if I piss you off now?

And then Tasos is screwed.

Proper done.

Gone.

So...

Keep your mouth shut malaka Vasilis.

Let him finish first to see what he wants.

And don't piss him off more than he already is." was his inner monologue. As a result, he didn't respond to Lupo and kept looking straight ahead.

"Look at me!" Lupo ordered him with a voice so sharp it could have cut glass.

Vasilis turned his head and finally looked at his biological father for the first time since he sat in the car.

"Let me be clear with you. Tasos will have to pay for what he did. Nobody fucks my wife. Nobody. But only you can save him." said Lupo.

"How?" asked Vasilis perplexed and, at the same time, frightened of what would come out of Lupo's mouth next.

"I want you to come and work for me. Right next to me. I'll teach you everything I know. You'll get to know the most important people in the country. And nobody will ever mess with you and your family. I guarantee this." proposed Lupo.

Vasilis' eyes widened and became glassy with fear. They couldn't focus straight ahead. His whole body sweated from top to bottom. His teeth were clenched so tightly that his jaw was aching. His ass tightened as if he was trying to hold back a tidal wave of diarrhoea. He was on edge, but he tried his best to hide it from Lupo.

Lupo continued: "I'm getting old. I want to get out soon. I have built a strong organisation Vasilis. I want you to take over when I'm gone."

"What about Lakis? He's your son..." asked Vasilis.

 "Lakis isn't cut for this. And he knows it. Don't worry about him. He's settled for life. He'll never have to work in his life if he doesn't want to. My offer is this: you start working with me and you get half a million euro for start. This is to support your family, so you don't have to work anywhere else. If this doesn't work for you, I'll do what I have to do with Tasos..."

"So basically, you try to buy me into working for you by blackmailing me. Because if I don't start working for you and take your dirty money, Tasos is gone. But this money's loads. I'll never make this money in a lifetime working at any normal shitty job here in Athens. And because of you being my father, I'll be a top dog in the mob straight away. But what happens if they want to get rid of me because I take another top dog's position waiting on the line to replace you? How will you guarantee my safety around all these blood-thirsty beasts? And will you forgive Tasos or wait for some time to pass and then you'll arrange for an accident to happen to him? You have to give me your word about it. Father to son. And if I say no to you now, how can I live with myself knowing that Tasos was killed because of my decision? Half a million euros just to start? What the hell! How much money do you have? And how much money will I make working with you if I start with half a mil? I'll live the life then! I'll never worry about money ever again." These were all the things he truly wanted to ask Lupo and wished he had the balls to say out-loud in the exact same way.

But he didn't.

This is how he responded instead: "If I start working with you, will you give me your word that nothing ever happens to Tasos? And I mean never ever. Will you?"

"I give you my word. Nobody touches Tasos." replied Lupo.

"Ok." said Vasilis and extended his right arm offering a handshake.

Lupo grabbed Vasilis' hand and pulled him towards him. He

then hugged him. This was his own way of establishing the deal with his son.

After the hug ended, Lupo said: "Go back inside now. I'm not going back there. Tell them it's all sorted. No more. Not a thing. Then take Tasos on the side and tell him to fuckin disappear from Athens. And stay away from Barbara forever if he wants to see another day. Because if he doesn't, no matter of our deal, he's fuckin gone. And then go next to Babis' ear and tell him not to worry about me. I knew everything about him and Lakis since day one, when they kissed at the park for the first time. I had tasked one of my men to keep an eye on Lakis so he's safe when he was out. He saved them from some pricks who threw stones at them."

"I'm not gonna lie; I was truly shocked from Babis' announcement. But to be honest, it all makes sense now. So many questions in my head are answered... I'm also surprised by your calm reaction to their relationship. I'm not quite sure if Soula sees this in the same way though ..." added Vasilis.

I'm very good at dancing like a bear

'Συνοικέσιο' (Synikesio): This word comes from the ancient Greek word 'synikeō', which means 'to live together'. It is made up of the words 'syn' (with, together) and 'ikeō' (to live).

In the Greek language, the word 'synikesio' was used to describe an agreement made between the families of two people, with the aim of sealing their marriage. This agreement usually included discussions about the financial status of the families, their social class and religious beliefs.

In the past, it was such a hard-core experience, especially for women, as they were promoted and 'traded' by their families like they were a piece of property. They had no say in the whole process and were forced to accept the man their family, usually the father, had chosen for them.

The father usually offered his daughter to the man's family in a form of a 'package deal'. This package included his daughter and a house or a plot of land or cash or animals or all of them together. The daughter was rated based on different factors like beauty and other external characteristics. The better looking the daughter, the smaller the 'package deal' was as this stock item (daughter) would go pretty fast.

Another critical factor was the age as a daughter older than twenty-five years old was carrying a significant risk, according to her family, *'na mini sto rafi'. (να μείνει στο ράφι). [literal translation: to be left on the shelf. This well-known is used to describe unmarried women. It originates from a longstanding Greek tradition where aged family heirlooms were displayed on shelves for decoration. Consequently, an unmarried woman of a certain age, was pretty much considered as a cherished family artifact.]* As a result, the older the daughter, the higher the package would be. Regardless of their economic status, it was a matter of pride for the fathers to be able to offer the right package along with their daughters.

In most instances where 'synikesio' occurred and resulted in arranged marriages, there were often unfavourable outcomes. The most common was domestic violence, as couples forced into marriage might lack the commitment necessary for a healthy relationship, making them more prone to abuse. As always, the main offender was the man. Another negative consequence was divorce. Several studies confirmed that couples in arranged marriages were twice as likely to divorce compared to those in love marriages. Finally, marriages from 'synikesio' often caused mental health problems among young individuals, usually women, who were coerced into marrying someone they didn't love, leading to depression, anxiety and other related issues, even suicide.

In modern Greece, 'synikesio' was less common, as young people now have more opportunities to meet and choose their partners on their own. It was a practice often seen as old-fashioned and undemocratic. But regrettably, it still existed in rural regions or in communities with traditional customs and practices.

Or as a last-resort measure.

"Maa, I don't wanna do this again! This is the third time now. I don't know how to make this clear to you. Why you never listen to me and you only do what you have in your head?" Babis asked Soula, rolling his eyes.

"Why? You know why. Because you're not getting any younger. And I want to see grandkids before I'm too old to enjoy them. All my friends already have grandkids. I'm the only one left without any. I can't look at them in the eyes sometimes from the shame I feel. And because you have never brought a woman to introduce her to me as your girlfriend. And with the way you eat all the time, you're not getting any slimmer. I'm not sure how you'll find a woman to marry you with all this extra weight you carry. You have destroyed your body with all the food you eat. And because you don't care about yourself, it doesn't mean that I don't care too. That's why!" Soula replied, fairly frustrated.

"Wow! Unbelievable! If you start, nothing stops you. Oh my God..." said Babis feeling unwilling to argue with her.

Soula sighed in desperation. "In the last month, you've already embarrassed me in front of the two women and their families I invited here for you to meet. They were so nice girls. Both of them. They would make such great wives and I could tell they would give me so many beautiful grandkids. And then you were out of control. All these crazy things you told them... I still don't even know what you were talking about. You made all of them wanting to jump out of the balcony to save themselves from all these silly things you said. I just don't understand why you did that. Do you want to make me die? Because that's what you'll do at the end. With all this pressure you give me, I'll definitely get a stroke. Or a heart attack like your father. And then I'll leave this world before I become a granny. My sweet boy! I'm begging you! Please give Kalliopi a chance. Her father has a lot of money and you'll be sorted for all your life. She's a good girl, very religious and I hear she's quite the cook. Think about it! "

"A cook? Mum, you just told me how fat I am and that I have 'destroyed my body with all this food'. And now you advertise her to me because she's a good cook? Are you serious?" replied Babis, raising an eyebrow.

"Get married and give me some grandkids and I swear to God I'll never say anything to you again about your body and how fat you are!" said Soula with the utmost seriousness. Then she looked Babis into his eyes: "Promise me that after we go back in the living room you will not embarrass me like the other times. I'm begging you!"

"And what about her moustache? It's almost as big as her father's." mentioned Babis mockingly.

"Shut up and move!" ordered Soula.

Babis just nodded, picked up the tray with the coffees and water glasses and walked out of the kitchen, towards the living room. Soula followed holding the tray with the cake slices.

Kalliopi was sitting on the sofa, between her mother and father. Babis reluctantly sat at an armchair across from Kalliopi and her family. Soula, being the highly hospitable host she was supposed to be, served everyone their cakes, coffees, and water.

Agamemnon, Kalliopi's father, began the conversation with authority in his voice. "Thank you for welcoming us into your home Soula. Before we begin, I want to make our intentions clear. I have great respect for our traditions and I believe my daughter, Kalliopi, would make an excellent match for your son Babis."

"Please, go on." suggested Soula, who was intrigued by what she just heard.

Agamemnon continued in the same authoritarian tone coming out of his mouth beneath his big, thick black moustache. "Babis, I've observed your independence and ambitions as a hardworking businessman. I highly appreciate a young man with serious goals in life. This is the kind of man you cannot find easily nowadays. Most young men have lost their values and don't follow our Greek traditions. They don't even believe in our God. And I don't even want to start about all these gay out there. But I see something different in you."

Soula, glanced at Babis, while Kalliopi's father continued speaking authoritatively. "There is a specific kind of man that every decent, Christian, young woman would love to have on her side to create a family. From my big experience in life and people, I can certainly say that you are one of this kind. So, it would be a blessing for our Kalliopi to get to know you better. And if you enjoy each other's company, why not be together and start a family? I assure you Babis, with our family's wealth and influence, you and Kalliopi will have a very comfortable life. I'm an old-fashioned man and I believe in providing for my daughter and her future husband."

Babis wanted to show that he was taken aback by the generous proposal and remained silent. Soula came to the rescue and asked in hesitation: "Well, Babis what do you think?"

"Thank you for your kind words, ehm... but marriage is not only about having a lot of money. I think love is more important than this." responded Babis seriously, keeping his frustration well-hidden deep inside him.

"I understand the importance of love in a marriage Babis and I assure you that Kalliopi is a woman of strong values and traditions. She will uphold her responsibilities as a wife." Agamemnon replied as firmly as possible.

Kalliopi blushed and adjusted her long skirt nervously, not knowing which direction to look at.

Soula turned towards Babis and said softly: "This is a great opportunity for your future, my Babis. Please think carefully about getting to know Kalliopi better. Why not go out for a date, just the two of you? I'm sure you'll have so many nice things to discuss!"

The room fell into a tense silence as everyone considered the weight of Babis' decision.

"Ok but I would like to know what Kalliopi thinks too." said Babis breaking the deadly silence in the room. "So, Kalliopi, you must be very religious."

"Yes, I am deeply religious. My Christian faith means everything to me." Kalliopi answered after she blushed for one more time. Finally, her voice reached the crowd for the first time since the meeting started.

Babis said after leaning in: "Well, I'm in love with..." He made a dramatic pause and continued: "...comic books. I believe in superheroes."

"Comic books? Superheroes? That's something you don't hear every day to be frank." Fritheriki, Kalliopi's mother, who was considerably confused, also spoke for the first time since they started the conversation.

"Oh, yes. I even want to start a superhero religion. The 'Super-Babis' religion. Would you like to join Kalliopi?" Babis asked the potential mother of his children and Soula's grandkids.

Kalliopi's eyes widen in disbelief, while her father was getting worked up.

"Babis, perhaps we could discuss more traditional matters, like family values." said Agamemnon trying to steer the discussion.

"Ehm... Ok. Of course, Mr Agamemnon. Ehm... Ok. I believe in family values. One big family value for me is that every family must have a pet." explained Babis.

"A pet?" Kalliopi asked puzzled.

"Yes. I love big fat snakes because one of them had bitten 'Super-Babis' and that's why he is a superhero now." replied Babis very seriously.

Babis last comment left Kalliopi's family feeling confused, exchanging bewildered glances with their eyes playing a game of ping pong. They weren't certain if he was joking or being serious. This uncertainty left them feeling rather peculiar.

"Babis! Please be serious for a moment." Soula asked him with a threatening stare, trying to rescue the situation.

"Ok mum. Ok. You're right mum. Ok. Ehm... Ok. Well. I want to tell the truth to all of you..." Babis said with a serious tone.

"What is it??" asked Kalliopi with hope in her voice.

"I'll join the circus next year. I don't like this life anymore and I don't want to have a restaurant. Ehm... So, I will sell it and work at a big circus. I'm very good at dancing like a bear. Do you want to see how good I am Kalliopi?" Babis remained dead serious all the time during his big announcement.

Kalliopi exchanged irritated looks with Fritheriki and Agamemnon, wanting to get everyone's attention, cleared his throat loudly. "Soula, we came here with sincere intentions. But with all the respect, your son's mockery is more than offensive.

"We expected a respectful meeting, but this is ridiculous. If you knew that your son isn't serious about getting married, you shouldn't have wasted our precious time. We have a very big business to run." Fritheriki added angrily.

"Mummy, can we please leave this place now?" Kalliopi asked with clear frustration and disappointment, with tears welling in her eyes.

"I'm so sorry for all this... I don't know what to say to you... Perhaps we can consider trying again in a few days once my Babis had more time to think about getting to know Kalliopi better. She's such a lovely woman. It's a shame to end it like this. Don't you think?" Soula tried to soothe this totally awkward situation.

Her charm didn't bring the expected outcome and the tension escalated. Kalliopi's family gathered their things and got up from the sofa, clearly annoyed and frustrated. "We cannot continue this conversation under these circumstances. And we'll never do this again. I promise you. Goodbye." Agamemnon expressed his disappointment just before they all left the meeting.

Soula was left speechless watching them exiting the flat and closing the door behind them. With tearful eyes and a heavy heart, she quietly left the living room without even looking towards Babis, with her footsteps echoing softly in the corridor. The weight of disappointment and humiliation caused by Babis' embarrassing behaviour could be heard with each step as she was heading defeated to her bedroom.

On the other side, Babis was experiencing mixed emotions. Part of him felt like a winner for dodging the marriage bullet for one more time and bringing the meeting to an early end. But at the same time, the guilt inside him was building up. He clearly understood that his behaviour was totally unfair for all the people around him. It wasn't really his style to act in such way and made him feel highly uncomfortable. But the strongest feeling of all was that he had reached the brink of exhaustion. All thanks to relentless Soula, who kept organising a parade of 'future wives' against his true desires.

Overwhelmed by these emotions, he found the flat suffocating and made a quick exit without any second thought. He headed down to the car park, got into his car and drove away. Tears were running down his face, this pressure was too high for him to bear any longer...

After a couple of minutes, when he had moved away from the neighbourhood, he called Lakis.

"Hey babe! Are you ok? How did it go? asked Lakis after he picked up the call.

"......" Babis couldn't speak a word; he was entirely lost in his tears. His sobs reached Lakis' ears on the other end of the call with perfect clarity.

"Are you crying my love??" asked Lakis again after he received no actual response from Babis, just the deafening sound of his pain.

Babis' voice trembled as he tried to respond amidst his heavy tears. "Lakis... I can't... No... I can't.... I can't take it anymore.... I'm about... to have a breakdown.... All this pressure is killing me..."

"I'm so sorry you had to go through this shit for one more time my love... But you won't have to do this ever again. I promise you; this was the last time my love." stated Lakis who was also crying softly.

"How Lakis?... What can you do?" asked Babis with traces of fresh hope in his words.

"I have made a big decision. Tomorrow, during my parents' 25th anniversary dinner at your taverna, I'll announce to them that I'm gay and we love each other my Babis." Lakis determinedly declared to the love of his life.

"You mean it?" Babis couldn't help but smile through his tears.

"Absolutely. We've been through so much babe. I can't stand seeing you like this. No more! Never again! That's it! It's time to show them how much you mean to me!" Lakis explained with a firm voice.

Babis wiped away his tears. "Oh my Lakis... I love you... But... What will your father say when he hears that you you're gay? And you love a man? Me... I'm really scared of him. I think he'll go mad and want to hurt us both. Also, how will my mum take this? She might get a stroke or a heart attack if I tell her I'm gay... And what about my taverna? Some customers will not want to come back again. I'm so scared for us my Lakis... What can we do?"

"We'll face all these together my love." Lakis replied with determination.

Babis was quick to answer. "Let's leave everything behind. Let's leave this country and live somewhere abroad. Somewhere we can be free for what we are... Please my love! Think about this! Let's leave this place forever..."

"No my love! We are not quitters! We'll fight with all our power! Love conquers all and I'm ready to fight for us until the end!" Lakis reassured him in a strong manner.

"So... this mean we're coming out?? Is this for real now??" asked Babis.
"Yes, my Babis! Yes! It's true! We're coming out my love!" replied Lakis.

"I'm so lucky to have you, my Lakis!" Babis' heart felt overwhelming gracefulness for his lover's consistently strong support.

"Forever and always my love." said Lakis with more tears now.

"Forever and always with you." responded Babis with fresh tears streaming from his eyes as well.

9:09pm, Thursday 13th May 2010

After Vasilis left the car to go back inside, Lupo made a phone call. He called two men waiting in a car parked close to his car. They were his bodyguards who were following him daily everywhere he went. In this case, due to the complexity of the issue and people involved, Lupo had instructed them to wait outside in their car until he called them.

"Drive me back. Then no more. Going out's off." Nikolas ordered them to follow him to the gate of his home and then they were free for the rest of the night as he wasn't going out as planned any more.

And that's what they exactly did when Lupo securely entered his property in his car. They drove away to enjoy whatever was left of the night.

Lupo had built a mansion on the outskirts of his childhood neighbourhood, determined to spend the rest of his days in the place he loved. It was located at the end of a winding private road, surrounded by a massive, tall fence. The steel bars were painted black and stretched up to the height of the surrounding trees, which had been strategically planted to cover the view from any prying eyes. The gate to the property was made of strong glimmering metal hinting at the wealth and power that lied beyond.

The gate was operated by a high-tech security system, with a camera in every corner outside. Anyone who approached the gate was scrutinized and only those with the proper credentials, who were known to Lupo and his family members, could be granted access. Once inside, a grand driveway was leading up to his imposing eight-bedroom mansion.

The house was impressive, with a large foyer that boasted a marble flooring and a crystal chandelier. The living room was adorned with luxurious leather sofas and there was a roaring fireplace that dominated one wall. The dining room was grand and spacious, with a long, polished wooden table that could seat up to twenty people. This is where Lupo had booked most of his biggest deals, while treating his guests with unforgettable eating and drinking experiences, usually by hiring top chefs and the most exquisite sommeliers from the city of Athens.

But it's the outside space that was out of this world. The property boasted a large, open area with a large pool surrounded by sun loungers and umbrellas. There's a large outdoor kitchen and dining area, completed with a built-in BBQ, perfect for hosting the couple's lavish parties.

The entire property was surrounded by lush gardens, with trees and flowers carefully selected to provide a sense of privacy and exclusivity. It was clear that this was a place of power and influence. The perfect sanctuary for a Mafia boss like Lupo, providing him and his family, both luxury and security in equal measure.

Barbara's car, a big black SUV, was parked outside, next to a white cabriolet sports car, that was Lupo's second car. His main one was a silver bulletproof compact luxury sports sedan, which he was using daily for transportation.

Since he spoke to Vasilis and made all the future arrangements, there was only one thing in his brain; what he should say to Barbara and how to react when he saw her again, after cheating on him with Tasos at the park.

"Should I play the fool?

Should I pretend that I know nothing about it?...

No.

Fuck it.

This is stupid.

Anyway, many people know about this already.

And I'll look like a fuckin idiot.

So...

I'll be open and honest.

This is the right way.

But how should I come across?

Angry?

Annoyed?

Betrayed?

Cheated?

Understanding?

Forgiving?

Revengeful?" were all the things going circles in his brain. Critical events had transpired in their relationship over the past year and he knew he had to be mindful of how he handled this sensitive topic with Barbara tonight.

Lost in his thoughts, he walked into their home. There's a deadly silence. Not a sound. The time was 9:14pm and Barbara should have been back home after her 'adventure at the park'. Based on the original plan, at 8:30pm both should have been already sitting at Babis' taverna with their son Lakis and Tasos with his family.

Lakis on the other hand, by sheer luck, got stuck with the rest of his friends in an extended drinking spree at another bar after Tasos left. He was running an hour late, and his estimated time of arrival at the taverna had moved to 9:30pm.

This meant one thing: the initial anniversary planning was in shambles by all sides.

"Barbara!" called Lupo.

No response.

He walked through their massive living room and investigated the kitchen.

No sign of her.

"Barbara!" he called again a bit louder, in case she was somewhere upstairs and couldn't listen.

Still no response.

He felt that something wasn't quite right. He walked quickly up the stairs to the first floor where all the bedrooms were located.

He went straight to their master bedroom.

No sign of Barbara.

But there was a folded piece of paper on his pillow.

'My Nikolas

Happy 25th wedding anniversary my dear!

How does it feel to be married to the same foolish woman for almost half of your life?

You wouldn't know because you never truly gave our marriage a real chance.

I still remember the day we met. I was so young and naive and so in love with you.

I thought I was the luckiest woman alive to have found a man like you, so brave and charming.

Little did I know then that I was going to get married to a lying, cheating, immoral, worthless cunt who doesn't deserve the air he breathes.

Last year, on this very day, I caught you fuckin with our housemaid.

On our 24th Anniversary...

I was devastated, humiliated and ashamed to have ever loved a man like you...

But with your tricks you managed to persuade me to stay.

What a fool I was...

Last week I realised that this was just the tip of the iceberg, wasn't it?

I feel so good that there're people in your team who really, and I mean really hate you.

These people revealed everything to me two days ago.

They told me that you've been cheating on me for years with every slut you met.

Which I could live with after the agreement we made a year ago in our unforgettable anniversary.

But what seriously destroyed me was the fact that you kept cheating on me in the last 12 months as well...

You pretend to be a Mafia leader, so rich and powerful, but you couldn't even keep your own house in order.

Well, I'm leaving you now.

I don't want to spend one more day with a liar and a cheat.

You never deserved a woman like me or any other woman who respects herself.

Don't bother trying to find me.

I don't want anything from you anymore.

Not your money, not your properties, not even any of your pathetic excuses for an apology.

I curse the day I ever met you.

I curse the day I said "I do."

I curse the day I allowed you to touch me, to "love" me, to break me.

You are a despicable human being and I hope you rot in hell.

P.S. Fucking like an animal with young men is my new favourite thing in the world.

"Your" Barbara'

Things will never be the same again my love

Barbara was in the living room, standing in front of the big sliding door leading to the garden. She was staring outside at the pool, which was sparkling in the sunlight, with a forced miserable smile on her face.

The preparations for their 24th wedding anniversary dinner had been planned to the slightest detail. By her. Only. For one more time, Lupo was too busy to get involved. He just picked and invited the guests this time.

The two executive chefs from one the most expensive restaurants in Athens were scheduled to arrive at 4pm to set up and complete all their preparations for the dinner to be served at 10pm. Greeks love to eat late.

Lupo was laying on their corner sofa looking at a printout of the highly exquisite menu Barbara had agreed with the two chefs. He had his reading glasses on and was fully concentrated to understand what was actually happening in it:

'Anniversary Dinner Menu

Date: Wednesday 13th May 2009

Guests: 12

Serving Time: 10pm

First Course

Greek Lobster Bisque with Crispy Fennel and Lemon Oil

Second Course

Seared Scallops with Taramosalata, Charred

Cucumber and Black Garlic

Third Course

Greek Salad with Tomatoes, Cucumbers, Feta Cheese, Kalamata Olives, Watercress, Candied Pecans and Orange Vinaigrette

Fourth Course

Grilled Mediterranean Sea Bass with Lemon and Oregano, Served with Roasted Potatoes and Artichokes

Fifth Course

Pan-Roasted Monkfish with Kalamata Olive Tapenade, Roasted Peppers and Lemon Confit

Sixth Course

Octopus with Chickpea Puree, Preserved Lemon and Chorizo Oil

Desserts

Trio of Baklava with Pistachios and Honey, Loukoumades (Greek doughnuts) with Lemon Curd and Greek Yogurt Panna Cotta with Fig Compote

"Do you believe they'll prepare all this food on time for 10pm, my love? asked Lupo after he finished reading the menu.

"They will. These two are the best in Athens. That's why they're getting one thousand euros each for the day." replied Barbara, still staring outside towards their pool.

"Only two thousand euros for a whole night? Isn't this a bargain or what? A chef is what I should have become." said Lupo very sarcastically.

"Do you believe you could have made a better deal with them? And let's not discuss how much you make a night and how you make it. Ok?" replied Barbara annoyed with his comment.

"Oh, my love! You can't take a joke! Come on now!" said Lupo and got up from the sofa throwing the menu on the glass coffee table in front of him.

He walked towards her and hugged her from behind. "Twenty-four years married today my sweet Barbara! I want us to have the best party ever!" He gave her a kiss on her right cheek and continued: "When's the DJ coming? I absolutely love this guy! He's the best one I have in the clubs. The customers go bonkers every night he plays."

"He'll be here at 7pm to set up and around 7:30pm he'll start." replied Barbara still looking outside.

"Come on girl, look at me." said Lupo and moved in front of her. "Is everything alright, my love? It's our special day today. If something's wrong, I need to know now."

Barbara had many thoughts she wanted to share with him, but she held back, feeling that the timing wasn't right. "Nothing to worry about, my Nikolas. I'm just thinking about our guests tonight."

Lupo had invited five men with their wives to celebrate their twenty-fourth anniversary in his luxurious mansion. Barbara wasn't too thrilled about the guest list though, as two of them were working for Lupo as his closest associates in his mafia group, the other two were ministers in the Greek government and the last one was the owner of the biggest petroleum company in Greece.

"So, who did you invite?" she asked and her voice laced with sarcasm.

"The usual suspects!" Nikolas replied, chuckling.

Barbara let out a sigh. "Great! Just what I wanted for our anniversary. A room full of shady criminals and their dull wives."

Lupo raised an eyebrow and said with a sardonic laugh: "They're my friends my love. And they're not criminals, they're just hardworking men like me!"

"Sure, they're not. I bet they all have squeaky clean records like you anyway. I love Greece so much! Live your myth in Greece babe!" exclaimed Barbara and rolled her eyes.

A playful chuckle escaped his lips, accompanied by a devilish glint in his eye. "Well, we all share the same level of cleanliness like the impeccably clear Greek blue sky. And they have all confirmed to me that they're coming. So, we better get ourselves ready to party tonight!"

Barbara just nodded. She was still not thrilled about this dinner party. She wished she could have chosen the guests this time.

She then wished all of them got involved in a car accident with minor injuries on their way there and therefore cancelled. Or even better, she felt sick in the following hour and she cancelled. As she struggled to prepare herself for the unbearable position she was going to face in the coming hours, the word 'cancel' floated into her mind like a promising sweet relief from this torturous experience. It was as if the universe was playing a cosmic joke on her, tempting her with this magic word like an ice-cold glass of lemonade on a hot Greek summer day, tauntingly just beyond her fingertips.

"How I wish my Lakis was here tonight! At least we could have a giggle with my sweet boy looking at all the walking encyclopaedias of stupidity who call themselves wives of the most important people in Greece... What a joke!" Barbara muttered silently to herself.

"Did you say something about Lakis? Did you speak with him today? How's his holiday in New York?" asked Lupo as he only heard Lakis' name from Barbara's monologue.

"Lakis is having the time of his life with his friends. He's coming back on Saturday my sweet boy. I miss him so much!" replied Barbara and looked at her diamond watch. "Oh shit! It's 1:45pm! Shit! I'm late for my appointment at 2pm with Eva. I must go now. It takes twenty minutes to get there. I'm leaving you now. See you in a bit. Bye!" Barbara gave Lupo a kiss at his left cheek and left in a hurry for her appointment with her hairdresser.

Lupo watched her perfect ass in the tight leather pants she was wearing, while she was walking away. After Barbara closed the main door behind her, he was left alone in their massive mansion, with a semi-erection.

Not entirely alone as their housemaid, Maria, was on duty, preparing everything for the night ahead. She was a twenty-five-year-old beautiful woman from Albania, who had had been working for them the last six months, just before Christmas 2008. Lupo, as always, never left such an opportunity to go missing, especially inside his palace.

He was having a secret affair with her for the last six months, which started shortly after she began working there. Lupo was a renowned and illustrious stallion without any patience, when it came to sticking his body parts in any hole available on a woman's body.

He walked into the laundry room where Maria was sorting out the washed clothes. He grabbed her from behind and pulled her into a passionate embrace. "I missed you, my naughty little bitch!" he whispered in her ear.

"Me too! I want you inside me babe! Now!" she replied, giggling, and lowered her pants, revealing the tinny thong she was wearing.

"Not yet. Follow me upstairs. We'll take a shower together first." Lupo pulled her pants back up. He then grabbed her hand gently and walked together out of the laundry room. They went up the stairs, hugging each other and giggling all the way.

Barbara was driving her big black SUV on her way to the hairdresser at a low speed, considering that she was already running late for her appointment. She was completely lost in her thoughts.

"I feel so lonely.

And I regret.

Twenty-four years married to a Mafia boss.

But it also feels like yesterday when I met you, my Nikolas.

My lovely Nikolas....

You always had all the time in the world for me...

Now you're always busy.

Am I just your trophy wife?

Only a symbol of your power and wealth?

Where's the passion we had when we were first married?

Is our relationship just a business arrangement?

I'm freaking out about your safety every day and night.

For years...

When will you be caught and sent to prison?

Or even worse, when one of your enemies kills you?

Will they kill you in front of me?

Or in front of our son?

Will they kill us all?

So anxious every moment.

....

Twenty-four years married to you.

And I feel so lost.

Where's the love we used to have?

How I miss the way you used to look at me...

The way your touch would send shivers down my spine...

Where are the days when we would spend hours talking and laughing together?

And yet, another fear haunts me.

Are you cheating on me?

This thought is lingering at the back of my mind.

All the late nights 'because of work'...

The secretive phone calls...

All the full days away from our home...

This is a pain that cuts me deep.

I cannot imagine a life without you, my Nikolas.

Is our love strong enough to keep us together?

I'm so confused.

Honestly, why am I still with you?

Is it because of the lifestyle?

Or because I love you?

Is it because you scare me?

Or because I'm scared for you?

Is it because of your power?

Is it because of your money?

Money...

Money?

Money!

....

Fuck!

Shit!

Money!!!

I forgot to get my purse!

Shit!

'Opios then ehi mialo, ehi podia...' (οποίος δεν έχει μυαλό, έχει πόδια). [literal translation: whoever has no brain, has legs. This Greek saying is used when the function of the brain isn't adequate in order to complete a specific activity successfully. Therefore, one ends up using different parts of their body, mainly the legs in the form of walking or running or any other necessary form, to manage to complete successfully the activity they had started.]

Barbara stopped the car on the side of the road, almost causing an accident with the car following her. She didn't care to the slightest about it. She just showed her middle finger to the man in that car behind her, who was cursing and beeping like a lunatic.

She then called Eva, the hairdresser, and informed her that she'll be late. Eva had no problem with it. Barbara was one of her favourite clients and she always paid extra for her services anyway. Barbara could skip paying for the hair styling as she could cover it next time. But she had a plan to collect and pay for a present she had ordered at a local jewellery shop for Lupo for their anniversary.

When she finished with the phone call, she turned the car around and drove straight back home. This time she drove very fast, reaching 130km/h in roads where the limit was just 50km/h. After six minutes, she was at the main entrance of their mansion. When she walked inside, she couldn't see Lupo in the living room where she had left him, but she didn't have the time to look for him.

"Nikolas!" she shouted once, but she received no response. She didn't really bother and ran up the stairs to go and get her purse from their bedroom.

As she entered the bedroom, she initially heard the shower running from their large en-suite bathroom. But she also heard some weird sounds coming out of there. It was kind of giggling, kind of sighing, kind of heavy breathing...

Without any second thought, she opened the door and stormed inside.

The sounds she had just heard came out of Lupo's mouth. Maria was in there with him, but she made no sound as her mouth was occupied by his penis.

"What the fuck is this???" she screamed.

Nikolas jumped off his position and Maria fell on her back. Barbara met the imposing sight head-on, with her gaze locking onto the towering figure of his penis. It was standing tall and firm, like an electric pole, looking her straight into the eyes.

"Barbara, I can explain..." said Lupo with a shaky voice like a kid who got busted red-handed stealing from his old man's pocket.

Barbara didn't want to hear any of it. She grabbed Maria from her hair while she was still on her knees and threw her forcefully to the opposite wall, landing there with the front of her face.

"You little Albanian bitch!" Barbara screamed at Maria, whose face was now covered in blood as she must have broken her nose after the crash on the wall.

"Get the fuck out of my house! Now bitch! Before I kill you! Get out!! Now!! Barbara screamed at her.

Maria jumped up, grabbed her clothes and disappeared out of the bathroom.

"Explain??? What to explain malaka? You're cheating on me bustard! After twenty-four years of marriage!" Barbara screamed at Lupo.

"Barbara, please calm down and listen to me..." said Lupo and tried to move closer to her.

"Don't touch me!" Barbara pushed him away with her eyes filled with tears of anger and betrayal. "I can't believe I've been living with a cheating scumbag for all these years..."

"Barbara, please listen to me..." Lupo tried to defend himself.

"I don't want to hear any of it!" she shouted back. "I'm leaving you Nikolas! I can't live with someone who doesn't respect me!" Barbara turned around and ran out of the bathroom.

Lupo, still naked, jumped out of the shower and ran like a cheetah to prevent her from leaving their bedroom. He managed to get to the bedroom door before her.

Now he was standing wet and naked between Barbara and the door. He quickly locked it and turned around facing Barbara. When he read Barbara's face, especially the look she gave him, he broke down.

Tears streamed down his red face.

"Barbara, please don't leave me... I'm an absolute malaka, but I love you. I'll do anything to make it up to you..."

"Get out of my way son of a bitch! And open the fuckin door!"

she screamed and pushed him violently on the door.

"Please my love, listen to me..." said Lupo and stretched his hands to hug her.

Barbara stroke both of his hands down and then she slapped him on the left cheek with all her power. "No malaka! You never touch me again!"

He was undoubtedly shocked by the force Barbara used to slap him. He looked back at her with his eyes wide open, full of surprise, anger and fear. It was the first time since he was a little boy that someone had physically assaulted him in such way.

He was left speechless.

He moved away from Barbara and stormed into his personal en-suite wardrobe.

"Where do you go now? Come back here and open this door! Now!" shouted Barbara still standing next to the door which she banged extremely hard with both of her hands.

There was no response from Lupo.

After ten seconds, he came back out of his wardrobe still naked. But now, he was holding his gun in his right hand.

Barbara froze completely.

He took a couple of steps closer to her and then stopped. He looked straight into her eyes and raised the gun slowly. He put it on his head and said: "If you leave me, I'll kill myself."

"Screw you Nikolas. You're bluffing like you always do. You'll never do that." replied Barbara mockingly, but fully shocked at the same time.

The deafening sound of a gunshot was heard just when Barbara completed her last word.

She bent forward and covered her face instinctively.

When she uncovered her eyes, she was totally horrified. She was certain that she would see Lupo down on the floor, lying in his own blood bath.

But he was still standing at the exact same spot without a

scratch.

"The next one will go straight through my brain." he said full of tears. "I'm honestly sorry for what I've done to you... There're no words to describe what an absolute malaka I am... But I love you Barbara and I can't live without you. Ask me anything you want to make it up to you. Anything... And I'll make it happen my love. As long as you stay with me... I need you in my life Barbara..."

Barbara's heart softened slightly, but she was still fuming. She quickly thought that this was an opportunity of a lifetime to secure herself for the rest her life. Anyway, she had permanently lost her trust in him, so she needed to act smart and take advantage of him, now that he was so vulnerable. She had to be practical rather than emotional in order to make the most out of this golden chance she was given.

"Anything Nikolas?" she asked.

"Anything. Just ask me." replied Lupo decisively in his desperation.

"I want twenty million Euro in my offshore account. And you swear that you never ever again go near any other bitch. Then I'll stay with you." she replied.

"Consider it done. Tomorrow the money will be in that account. And I swear I'll never have sex with another woman until I die. I'll do anything to keep you by my side my Barbara!"

For the second time since this battle had started, he stretched his hands to hug her. This time Barbara didn't strike them down. She reluctantly made a couple of steps forward and let him hug her. Then, she hugged him too.

"Things will never be the same again my love. I promise you." he whispered in her ear while he was hugging her firmly.

Lupo's behaviour was 'na se heso Yianni, na se alipso meli'. (Να σε χέσω Γιάννη, να σ' αλείψω μέλι). [literal translation: First, I will have a shit on you Johny, then I will rub you with honey. This Greek proverb offers a life lesson, meaning that it makes no sense *to try afterwards to soften the consequences of your horrible actions.]*

He was right. Things would never be the same. Only for Barbara though. She was mentally broken after that day. She would never feel the same about him ever again. There was a big crack in her heart now and her trust in him was seriously damaged.

On the other side, things stayed the same for Lupo. He continued having sex with any female available. Maria the housemaid included.

Just with some extra caution.

9:24pm, Thursday 13th May 2010

Barbara's letter fell from Lupo's hands when he finished reading it. He was devastated with what he had just read. It was impossible to believe she was gone from his life. He just couldn't imagine life without her.

He completely lost the ground under his feet. He felt sick in the stomach and his head was pressing like it would explode. His heart was pounding and had difficulty in breathing. He was heading towards a severe panic attack.

He leaned on the chest of drawers next to the bed and took some deep breaths. He then raised his head and looked at his reflection in the mirror. He continued breathing deeply and slowly, staring at himself.

"Who the fuck are you old man?

A cheater?

A liar?

A hypocrite?

How did you expect Barbara to respect you?

You don't even respect yourself.

You bastard.

You're a disgrace to your own family name.

What's wrong with you?

You goddamn monster.

You can't even keep your own wife happy.

You pathetic excuse for a man.

You wonder why she left you...

How did she put up with you for so long?

What kind of a man are you?

How could you let this happen?

How could you make the one person who stood by you through thick and thin, go?

And for what?

Because you couldn't keep your goddamn hands to yourself?

Because you were so weak to keep your dick inside your pants?

Why didn't you treat her better?

Where have you been when she needed you, malaka?

You were out there chasing pussies.

And fucking women like a goddamn animal.

You stupid little man.

How can you ask for her forgiveness now?

How can you find anything to make it up to her?

One year ago, you promised her you would never cheat again.

But you couldn't help yourself...

You're such a scumbag.

...

...

And those backstabbing sons of bitches.

How could they do this to me?

People from my own team.

I trusted them with my life.

I made them what they are.

And they betrayed me.

The ungrateful bastards.

I trusted them and they stabbed me in the ass.

These pricks.

I swear to God.

When I find out who spoke to Barbara...

They will wish they were dead.

They'll suffer like they've never suffered before.

They'll fuckin pay.

They'll see what happens when they mess with me.

They think they can get away with this...

The cunts.

They'll regret the minute they're born.

...

But wait old man.

Is it entirely their fault?

Maybe you brought this on yourself, malaka.

Maybe if you had been a better man...

Maybe if you had kept your promise...

She would still be here with you.

You stupid malaka.

What do you do now?

How do you fix this now?

Can you even fix this?

Is it too late?

Why don't you know what to do?

You always know what to do.

Why are you lost now?

I hate you.

I hate you for everything you've done.

I hate you for driving her away.

I hate you for not being able to control your spoilt self.

I hate you for being a weak, pathetic man.

I can't even look at you in this fuckin mirror!!"

'*I maimu ithe ton kolo tis ke tromaxe*'. (Η μαϊμού είδε τον κώλο της και τρόμαξε) [literal translation: the monkey saw its ass and got frightened. This graphic greek saying refers to those who *realize and show late interest in a serious defect of theirs by being massively surprised because they had never spent the necessary time to reflect on their horrible behaviour and its impact on others.]* His reaction was instinctive. He punched the mirror in front of him with almost all his power, shattering it into a thousand pieces. He then pushed everything away from the top surface of the chest of drawers. Barbara's make up and beauty items, along with shattered pieces of glass from the mirror, all scattered and fell to the floor around him. He was acting like a total nutjob, ready to obliterate anything in his damn way.

Lupo had officially entered the 'Wild Maniac Rampage' mode.

"I need to find her.

But where's she now?

...

Only Olga will know.

She's her best friend.

She must know.

But if I call the bitch, she won't answer.

I'll go straight to her house.

Now!"

Being still dizzy and unstable, he turned around to get out of the bedroom. As the floor was full of debris from the destruction he had just caused, he stepped on a big piece of glass from the smashed mirror. His right foot slipped on it, causing him to completely lose his balance.

Lupo landed on his face on the corner of their extra king-size bed and then his whole body crashed down on the marble floor. The fall was spectacular and the impact exceptionally strong. But his adrenaline was so high that he felt almost nothing and got up straight away.

His eyes fell on the full body mirror standing on the wall in front of him. He went closer to check what had happened as he felt something was wrong inside his mouth. He could see blood running from his lips down to his neck.

When he opened his mouth, he completely lost it; three of his top incisors were gone as he landed on them on the bed frame.

Not chipped.

Completely gone.

This left him with a ridiculous hole when he opened his mouth. He looked like a bloody toothless vampire out for a kill.

He turned around and checked the floor next to where he fell. What he saw were his three front teeth lying there. It was official. He had reached his lowest point.

Ever.

He went ballistic.

He turned around again and kicked this mirror with his right leg, smashing it as well. Now the bedroom looked like a tornado had swept through it.

With his adrenaline having exceeded the highest safety limit, he walked out of the bedroom without the slightest concern about his bleeding mouth. All he wanted was to find Barbara. His brain was fixed on this and no amount of blood could stop him.

He burst into his office and went straight to the safe behind the office chair. His hands were shaking so badly that it took him four tries to enter the combination correctly. He was still in shock from what had just happened. When the door of the safe was finally open, he took two things out of it: his handgun and also, his 'dark' secret. He had kept this so well-hidden that literally nobody knew about it. If someone ever found out about it, that would be an absolute disaster.

This was his teddy-bear.

He had it since he was three years old, a present from his father. He used to call it 'Baba' because it always reminded him of his dad. 'Baba' was wearing a t-shirt with the follow phrase typed on it: 'Baba Loves Nikolas'.

Lupo secretly spoke to 'Baba' very often, especially when he was under pressure. He was confessing all the wrong things and crimes he committed, always asking 'Baba' for his forgiveness and understanding. Every time he spoke to 'Baba', he felt like his dad was listening and offering his forgiveness to him at the end.

He held 'Baba' with both of his hands and looked into its eyes. But this time he couldn't say a word. He just cried. The same way he used to cry in front of his daddy when he was beaten by the older kids.

This time, he was beaten by himself.

"I'm sorry 'Baba'... I have to go and make things right... This time you have my word... I will."

He placed 'Baba' back in the safe and locked it. He picked up his gun and a set of car keys. He decided not to take his bulletproof sedan as he wanted to drive as fast as possible to Olga's house. He got out of the house and went straight into his white cabriolet sports car, still looking like a toothless vampire who had just drank someone's blood from their neck.

It was a typical Thursday evening in his neighbourhood, quiet and uneventful. The streets were almost deserted and the only sounds were the occasional barking of a dog or the distant hum of passing cars.

Lupo shattered the tranquillity of the scene with his car, roaring through with lightning speed and deafening noise. He reached 160km/h in streets where the speed limit was 50km/h. He didn't stop at any red lights. He just kept on driving. It was as if he was playing Russian roulette with other car drivers who would be unfortunate enough to find themselves on his way. He only wanted to reach Olga's house as fast as possible no matter the cost. His emotions had completely conquered him.

He entered a one-way street and accelerated his car to the max. Just before he passed another red light, a small red car came out of a corner and stopped at the red light just in front of him. Lupo stepped on the brakes at the last minute and just managed to avoid crushing at the rear side of this car.

He was furious with this development. He cursed unstoppably and banged the driving wheel with both of his hands. When the light turned green again, he beeped continuously and lowered his window simultaneously.

"Eh malaka! Don't thtop! Move! Fuckin move! Go! Thtupid bathtard go! For fuck'th thake!" he shouted at the red car driver in front of him with both his head and left hand completely out of the window. Another little issue he had was that he couldn't say the letter 'S' with his three front teeth lying on his bedroom floor.

The small car didn't move an inch. Its dark tinted windows, which looked like mirrors, made it impossible to see what was going on inside it.

Out of nowhere, a black adventure touring motorcycle, with two passengers approached his car with high speed from behind and came to a sudden stop next to his right front window. Lupo was busy shouting at the people in the front car blocking him, so he didn't notice them.

Both riders on the black motorbike were fully dressed in black and had black helmets on, with black tinted face shields. The passenger in the back was holding a military automatic rifle. When Lupo sensed the mortal danger and tried to reach for his gun, it was already too late.

He received a barrage of fire from the black riders from hell.

The sound of the automatic rifle echoed through the deserted street at a deafening level. When done, both the small red car and the motorbike fled the scene at breakneck speed.

Lupo was dead.

He was laying lifeless inside his car with blood spurting like a fountain from different parts of his body. Three out of the twelve bullets that hit him went straight through his head.

His death was instant.

It was 9:48pm, on Thursday 13th May 2010.

Moments after the deadly attack, people in the area began to gather on their balconies to see what had happened. In one of these balconies, an elderly man turned to his ten-year-old grandson and said: "My little boy, always remember; *Opios anakatevete me ta pitura, ton trone I kotes."* (όποιος ανακατεύεται με τα πίτουρα, τον τρώνε οι κότες). *[literal translation: whoever gets mixed up with the bran, gets eaten by the hens. By using this expression, Greeks mean that whoever gets involved with things of dubious quality and ethics, will be irreparably damaged at the end...]*

The police investigators who arrived at the scene found eighteen shell casings scattered around the area of the deadly attack. They launched an official investigation, but off the record, they knew very well that this murder was a Mafia hit. Lupo was a known Mafia boss and they knew without the need of any further investigation that this was a revenge killing.

8:15pm Monday 12th May 2011

The veranda of the villa in Porthoussa, a small Greek island, perched high above the Aegean Sea. It was the perfect spot to witness the breath-taking Greek sunset. As the sun slowly descended towards the horizon, it painted the sky with hues of orange, pink, and purple, casting a warm glow over the landscape below.

A woman, looking as if she's been transported straight out of a travel magazine, was lounging on a deck chair. The look on her face was showing that she had no care in the world, while she was sipping on a glass of ice-cold wine. The gentle lapping of the waves against the shore and the distant cry of seagulls were the only sounds to be heard in this idyllic Aegean landscape.

As the sun was sinking lower to the horizon, the hues became more vibrant, making the sky look as if it caught fire. As she took in the stunning vista, she couldn't help feeling a sense of awe washing all over her body. It was impossible for her to believe that such beauty existed in this corner of the world. Moments after, the sky darkened and the colours faded away, the cool evening breeze picked up and sent a shiver down her spine.

Suddenly, a rustling sound caught her attention and she turned around to see a shadowy figure moving slowly towards her.

"Who the hell is this now?

I didn't invite anybody here.

And everyone's busy for tomorrow." she thought.

But then the figure stepped into the light. It was just the villa owner, coming to check on her.

"Is everything ok Mrs Barbara? Isn't it beautiful here? I have lived in this villa for decades and every single time this view excites me like the first time!"

"All is good Mr Manolis. Thank you." replied Barbara.

"What about tomorrow? Have you arranged everything? Please let me know if you need help with anything. You know, we never had an event like this in our small island before. I hope all goes well. Some locals are a bit 'nervous' with the whole thing, to say it politely. I honestly wish it all goes well and you all have the best time tomorrow!"

"They better mind their own business, tell them. And thank you for your kind words, Mr Manolis." replied Barbara and took another sip of her wine.

"I totally agree Mrs Barbara. Enjoy the rest of your stay in our small island!" he said and walked away, leaving Barbara alone again.

As the night settled in, she continued sitting on the breath-taking veranda, lost in her thoughts and wonder. This sunset had been one of the most beautiful things she had ever seen. She felt grateful to have witnessed it in such a tranquil and calm setting, just one day before her son Lakis would exchange vows on a dreamy beach with the love of his life, Babis.

Looking out at the vast expanse of the Aegean Sea, she travelled one year back, the day her Nikolas was murdered. As she gazed out at the peaceful waters, her thoughts drifted back to that fateful day.

"It's been a year since I lost you, my Nikolas.

And the pain still feels raw.

Your murder on our twenty-fifth anniversary still haunts me every day.

Every bloody day...

When they told me about it...

I can still feel the heat of the tears rolling down my face.

The way my heart pounded as I screamed your name.

I still can't believe how badly things turned out for you and me.

I knew you were a cheating lying bastard.

But I never stopped loving you.

I miss the true Nikolas so much.

I still remember the way he used to laugh.

The way he used to hold me.

The way he used to make me feel.

The way he used to make me feel alive.

And now all of that is just a distant memory.

I can't stop blaming myself for what happened to you that day.

If I hadn't left you...

...

And your funeral...

Your funeral...

The biggest event of the year.

All these famous fuckers.

All the scumbag politicians.

Paying their respects to a 'friend' who had the highest of virtues and ethics.

How disturbing it was to watch them offering their condolences to their 'virtuous and ethical friend'.

The level of insincerity and hypocrisy on display...

What a silly circus...

I felt so alone amongst thousands of people.

...

But tomorrow is a special day.

Our Lakis will become one with his love for life.

I'm so happy and blessed for our son.

It's a reminder that life goes on.

That there is still love and happiness to be found.

I know Nikolas, you would have been proud of our son.

I can almost hear you cheering in the background.

I'll never forget you, my Nikolas.

My true Nikolas.

Even if you were a proper malaka at the end.

I know you would want me to be happy.

To live my life to the fullest.

And this is what I'll continue doing until I die."

Barbara sighed as her heart was heavy with all the memories. Since Lupo's murder, she had been travelling solo around the world, without staying in the same place for more than four weeks at the longest. She had visited friends she had in different places in the world, but during each trip, she also discovered new friends and experiences that filled her with joy and wonder.

She was a traveller at heart, journeying across the world to explore new places and make unforgettable memories. She travelled all around the globe, to fulfil her childhood dreams, including beautiful places in all continents like the Bhutan's mountains, Fiji's tropical paradise, New Zealand's rugged landscapes, Iceland's stunning scenery, Morocco's bustling markets, and ancient wonders in Myanmar and Peru.

But the feeling she experienced the last few days in this tinny Greek Island in the centre of the Aegean Sea, had made her want to settle there. It looked like a paradise on earth to her. Its idyllic beauty, raw simplicity and serene charm captured her soul. She knew inside her that she had found her perfect base to escape from everything and everyone. And whenever she would feel the urge to explore new places, she could simply follow her heart and wander wherever it led her. For the new Barbara in the ALD (After Lupo's Death) era, life was all about adventure, freedom and the joy of giving-no-shit.

Her thoughts were interrupted by the sound of a car pulling up outside. From her veranda, she looked down to the quiet and lacking any traffic road, to see Vasilis, Babis' brother, stepping out of a blue van with a logo 'VVIP Events' (*Very*

Very Important People Events) on the side.

After Lupo's murder, Vasilis concentrated on his new girlfriend, Eleni, and the VIP events business he started with her, seven months ago. They had both organised everything for the event on the remote beach the next day, when Lakis and Babis would finally become one.

"Hey Barbara, how're you? It's been such a long time since I last spoke to you!" said Vasilis excitedly when he reached the veranda, where Barbara was enjoying her wine looking at the magic beauty of the Aegean Sea.

Barbara didn't answer to him. She walked towards his direction and gave him a warm hug with a kiss in both cheeks. He responded in the exact same way.

"Vasilis my dear! It's so nice to see you after a whole year!"

"I feel exactly the same! Last time we spoke was during Nikolas' funeral..." replied Vasilis.

"I know, I know. What an absolute shit-show my Nikolas funeral was... All these people there pretending to be sad for him... Bullshit Vasilis, total bullshit. You see, he was very well known and deeply connected. But I wish his funeral was only for the few people who truly loved him. Truly cared about him. And as far as I know, you are one of them. Isn't it true?" asked Barbara looking straight into his sad eyes.

"It's true Barbara, indeed. Nikolas was someone I was looking up to since I remember myself. Growing up in the same neighbourhood with someone like him... That was a massive influence for me. But the day he died... I'm sure you must have heard about it as well. I found out that he was my biological father. And then he was gone... An hour after we spoke and agreed on a few things, he was killed. Still can't process it in my head..." Vasilis paused, staring at the floor.

He then raised his head and said: "I'm truly sorry you had to find out about Nikolas being my father like this..."

"Listen to me my sweet boy. From all the cheating I suffered from him, this is the only thing that never bothered me. To be honest, I feel blessed that he contributed in his own unique way to bring a man like you in this world. I respect your mother Soula. She's a very descent woman. She never brought any trouble to my relationship with Nikolas. And I know you since you were born. I always admired your character, your personality. And now I know why. You have him inside you. But I wish you got his good side. Because he also had a very dark side my boy..." said Barbara.

"I would like to reveal something to you. I haven't spoken to anyone about it. The day he was killed, we agreed that I would start working with him so he wouldn't harm Tasos for what happened between you and him earlier that day. He offered me a big amount of money to start as well. He wanted me next to him. I was horrified only with the thought I would be working for the Mafia... When I heard about his death I was devastated. But the bloody truth is that I was also relieved. I couldn't see myself being happy in there. It wasn't for me. I feel like shit for saying this, but it's the truth. I just wanted to take this out of my chest..." Vasilis was now looking straight down to the floor, feeling truly guilty for his feelings.

"Don't Vasilis. Please don't. Nikolas, as caring and protective he was, he also had the devil inside him. I don't blame you. You never wanted his death. What you wanted was your life. Never forget this." responded Barbara.

Vasilis raised his eyes filled with tears and hugged her. She did the same.

"Ok, ok. Enough with Nikolas. Let's discuss about something happy. Tell me about your new girlfriend!" said Barbara after hugging him.

"Oh, Eleni! I'm so lucky I found her!" replied Vasilis with his wet eyes sparkling of joy now. "She managed to turn my life upside down in the last eleven months. I met her when I was in my real lows and I felt like she was godsend. She's beautiful, she's bright, she's sensible, she's sensitive, she's funny, she's firm. I love her Barbara! I love being around her, working with her, spending time doing nothing with her! Sometimes I struggle to believe that I found someone like her!" replied Vasilis excitedly.

"That's so sweet! I'm so happy for you! It's so hard to feel like this for anyone in life. I truly wish it stays this way my boy! You truly deserve it. Why didn't you bring her with you tonight? I would love to meet her."

"Thank you so much for your kind words Barbara! She had to stay with Soula tonight as she wasn't feeling very well, after the long ferry trip from Piraeus today. You'll have the chance to meet her tomorrow anyway."

"That's cool! Looking forward to it! So, tell me about Soula. How's she with the whole thing for tomorrow?" asked Barbara."

Vasilis took a step back, looked at the sky and sighed, revealing his emotional fatigue with this topic.

"I'm not going to lie to you. She continues to pray daily for Babis to rediscover the path of Jesus and to find a woman to have children. Preferably a virgin with good cooking skills to cover his strong appetite. But a 'partially used' one will also do the trick for her. This is an extreme case here for Soula and she can slightly compromise her standards."

They both looked at each other for two seconds and burst out laughing. They laughed, and laughed, and laughed... They both needed this laugh.

"Oh, bless her! That's brilliant Vasilis! I don't remember when it was the last time I laughed so much to be honest!" said Barbara still laughing with his comment.

"I know! Poor Soula! She's been through a lot. I can't seriously hold this against her. To be fair she's trying very hard in her own way to hide it. But if you know her, it's so clear that she's not comfortable with the whole situation. But can you entirely blame her? Being so religious and taking seriously all these Orthodox priests with their hate speech, led her to this point." exclaimed Vasilis with high emotion. "But she loves Lakis and she can clearly see how happy they both are together. So, even if her head is pretty messed up with the whole thing, I'm confident that her brain function has already changed towards the right direction. She just needs her own time with it I believe."

"I do understand. And I totally agree with you. We all need to respect her thoughts and feelings. This will help her to accept what we expect from her. But enough with the past. Let's discuss about the future now. Tell me about tomorrow. Is everything ready?" asked Barbara.

"I must give it to both! The beach they chose is one of the best I've ever seen in my whole life! It's an actual bitch to get to and set up, but it worth's all the effort. I'm so proud of Eleni and the rest of my team for pulling this through. So, we'll create a simple and elegant altar with flowers having all the colours from the rainbow. This will be placed almost where the waves crash. White chairs will be arranged in a semi-circle for the thirty guests under a shade structure made of different silks. We hired a local restaurant for the food and the menu is mainly based on grilled fish, Greek salads, and fresh fruits. About the drinks, we have brought with us one of the best mixologists in Athens to serve his out-of-space cocktails. The DJ is one of the best in Athens, a top woman this one. The boys have also requested a playlist of their favourite songs for the reception. Fireworks display is on as well. As the night draws to a close, this will be such a memorable way to end the evening and leave a lasting impression on all of us. And finally, there will be a surprise act."

"Now you know you need to tell me what the surprise is!" Barbara looked at him with a cheeky smile on her face. "Come on Vasilis! We revealed so many things tonight, this last one won't hurt anyone, believe me! I won't say anything to anyone. I promise you!"

"Ok, ok. Well. The boys have dreamt of a Magical Fire Show for their party. After they have exchanged their vows, we have arranged for a professional fire performer to put on a dazzling fire show during the party. This woman is amazing! She'll use a variety of props such as fire fans, poi and staffs to create mesmerizing patterns of fire in the air. She'll also use coloured flames and wear a costume that matches the wedding colours!" explained Vasilis in full excitement.

"Oh, my two lovelies! It all sounds fantastic Vasilis! Well done! Honestly, I can't wait for tomorrow! I love them both so much! They're such a matching loving couple!" exclaimed Barbara emotionally.

"I love them with all my heart too! I'll do my best with my team to make tomorrow's day unforgettable for everyone, especially them too. They truly deserve it!" agreed Vasilis. "Well, I must go back to my Eleni now. It's getting late and we have a long day ahead. Come here!" Vasilis hugged Barbara and gave her a kiss on each of her cheeks, the proper Greek way. She returned the hug and kisses too.

"Thank you for everything my Vasilis! Nikolas would have been extremely proud for the man you have become. Let's enjoy our boys' celebration of love tomorrow! Goodnight my boy!" said Barbara as she sent him off.

While the sun set over Porthoussa island, the two lovebirds nestled in a luxurious villa, eagerly anticipating the dawn of the biggest day of their lives.

The air was thick with excitement, their hearts beating wildly in anticipation of what was to come. With every passing moment, their passion grew more intense, like a spark igniting a fire that could not be contained. It was a night they would never forget, filled with love, desire, and the promise of a future together. But little did they know, their journey was just getting started...

"Did you just fart?! Are you a malaka now??" exclaimed Lakis with a fake grin plastered on his face, leaping in disgust off the bed he was lying with Babis.

"No, I didn't! Did you?" replied Babis pretending to be fully surprised.

"For God's sake Babis! It smells like someone just opened a

plastic tub with a rotten lobster, left outside the fridge for two weeks! Gross!! Ewwww!!!" shrieked Lakis with disgust.

"Is it maybe because we both ate a full lobster each for lunch? Don't you think babe??" asked Babis sarcastically as he laughed out loud. "Come on, admit it. It was you babe! The first who smells the fart is the farter, you know this!"

"Oh, you filthy cheeky bear! You're in real trouble now!" yelled Lakis and jumped back next to Babis.

They both whooped with laughter as Lakis tickled Babis all over his body. They were frolicking around like a couple of overly enthusiastic little boys on a scorching summer day wearing only their underwear. The cheerful sound of their giggling escaped the opened veranda door and could be heard from far away as it was breaking the peaceful evening silence in this part of the island.

"Oh stop! Stop Lakis! Stop! Please! I can't breathe!" begged Babis who was out of breath from all the relentless tickling he received from the love of his life.

"Only if you don't fart again! Because if you do, you won't live to see tomorrow! I give you my word!" Lakis threatened Babis, trying not to laugh at the same time.

"I swear my love! I swear that I won't fart again tonight! I swear to your life my love!" Babis responded.

They both burst out laughing with Babis sacred promise. When they finished with the intense laughter, they locked eyes. Babis wrapped his arms tightly around Lakis' waist while they laid together on the bed, enjoying the warmth of each other's embrace. They had been together since they were fifteen years old and yet every moment spent with one another still felt like the first.

Babis turned his head to gaze at Lakis' eyes, lost in the beauty of his smile. "Can you believe it's tomorrow?" he said softly.

Lakis smiled and kissed him on his forehead. "I can hardly wait my love!" he said. "It's been such a long time coming..."

Babis sighed contentedly, feeling a sense of peace and

happiness washing over him. "Do you remember when we first kissed at the park?" he asked.

Lakis chuckled. "How could I forget? I was so nervous, I thought I was going to faint."

"Me too! We were both so young and innocent." said Babis and smiled with this memory.

"Do you remember those little assholes who came afterwards? They almost killed me with that stone..." said Lakis still feeling upset from that incident.

"How could I forget..." answered Babis.

"And then... How lucky we were when that man came out of nowhere? He's our guarding angel. Like someone sent him to protect us. God bless him wherever he is." Lakis continued with tears welling up in his eyes.

Babis squeezed Lakis' waist reassuringly. "Oh, my Lakis! Let's forget about those bastards. How many times people said things about us? For what we are... For loving each other... But we grew up together. And we are still in love!"

Lakis nodded while tears were running down his face. "I never thought I could feel this way about anyone," he said. "But with you, it's like everything just makes sense. You complete me my love!"

Now Babis felt his own eyes filling with tears. "You complete me too my Lakis! And tomorrow, we make our love official to all the world." said Babis wiping the tears from his face. "I love you so much!"

"I love you too!" Lakis whispered, pulling him even closer. "Forever and always."

"Forever and always." Babis repeated.

As they drifted off to sleep with their hearts full of love and anticipation, they knew that tomorrow would be the start of a new chapter in their lives. One that would be filled with joy, laughter and a love that would never fade.

Forever and always

The big day had finally arrived. One exact year after Lupo's murder, Lakis and Babis had decided that this would be the best date to make their love official and pay their respects to his memory.

But Soula had a bad feeling about this date from the first time they informed her about their plans. She had repeatedly warned both Babis and Lakis not to exchange vows on Tuesday the 13th, a cursed day, a very unlucky one.

She had told them that on a Tuesday the 13th in 1453, the Fall of Constantinople, a.k.a. Istanbul, took place by the Ottomans. She also told them that the sum of the date 1453 is the number thirteen. Double-evil-stay-away date in her own words.

But they both ignored her. They knew this was one of the authentic Greek superstitions she strictly believed in and had busted everyone's balls about throughout the years. Here's the list with the rest:

A. Mati (the Evil Eye): In Greece, there's a belief that someone can cast a spell on you with their envious gaze, which is referred to as 'the evil eye' or 'mati'. If you're unlucky enough to catch this curse, you'll feel like crap both physically and mentally. It's like a hangover, but without the fun of drinking first. Luckily enough, there are experts in 'xematiasma' or 'the undoing of the eye', who can save you from this terrible fate. You can call up one of these specialists, (Soula was a master in it) to say a special prayer and release you from the pain inflicted by the evil eye. To remain 'potent', the cure for the evil eye must be handed down across the genders (a woman teaches a man who teaches a woman etc). It's like playing a game of broken telephone, but instead of a silly message getting garbled, you're getting rid of the bad juju.

B. Spitting. The Greeks' unique way of chasing away bad luck, misfortune and even the devil himself. When they want to protect someone from these evils, they just give them a good spit. It's like telling the devil: 'Hey malaka devil, there's nothing valuable here, so get lost!' It's not uncommon to see loved ones showering babies with copious amounts of spit to keep them safe. But it's not just the little ones who need protection. If someone compliments your looks, you'll need to spit three times to avoid getting cursed with 'mati' (see No1). And when it comes to hearing bad news, the Greeks will give a little spit while saying 'Ftou' three times to chase away any misfortune that might come their way. It's like touching wood to avoid bad luck, but in a more liquidy version.

C. Sneezing. The act of sneezing had a prophetic significance in Ancient Greece. It was believed to be a message from the Gods about an unseen future. In modern Greece, it has become a prevalent superstition, which suggests that sneezing implies someone is speaking about you. To identify the culprit, you can ask your fellow companion for a three-digit number and add up the digits. The resulting number will correspond to a letter of the alphabet, revealing the person who is criticising you negatively behind your back. For instance, if the numbers given are three, four and five adding them would result in twelve, which corresponds to the twelfth letter of the alphabet, L. Hence, the one talking about you can be a Lydia or a Lysandros or a Lilia or a Laurentios or a Lysistrati or a Lazaros or a Lenia or a Leandros or a Lefteris or a Lena or a Leonidas or a Leonora or a Leontios or a Lukia or a Loulis or a Litsa or a Lukas or a Lucretia or a Lukianos or a.........

D. Offer a perfume as a gift. Don't. It will cause irreparable harm to your Greek friendship and in order to counteract this catastrophe, the gift-receiver must give a coin of any value back to the gift-giver.

E. Handing a knife to someone. If you want to remain friends with this someone in Greece, you must avoid handing them a knife directly. Instead, you should place the knife on a table or surface and allow them to pick it up themselves. If you fail to follow this, say adios to your friendship, probably with all the drama included.

F. Leave from the same door you came in. It's a must. You need to make sure that your Greek guests leave your house through the same door they entered. If they make the mistake to leave through a different door, it's bad luck and will cause the breakup of a romantic relationship of people from your close environment.

G. Black cat = shit luck. If you see one, say 'FTOU' immediately and then spit. For further instructions see No2: 'Spitting'.

H. 'Yia Mas!' with coffee. No, no, no. You can say 'Yia Mas!' with ouzo, tsipouro, whisky, wine, beer and any alcoholic beverage. But if you try it with coffee... God save your soul.

Babis and Lakis had managed to overcome the obstacle called 'Soula's superstitions' and made the necessary peace in their minds about changing vows on a 'cursed Tuesday the 13th'. Their only concern was how everything they had imagined for the event on this special day would become reality and come nicely into place. And that's where Vasilis showed his real value. With his team, they had organised everything, from A to Z, to make this day unforgettable.

The remote beach chosen by the couple for the exchange of their vows was surrounded by rocky cliffs and outcrops, providing an amazing contrast to the soft & golden sand that stretched out before the ceremony spot. The sun had begun dipping toward the horizon, casting a warm and golden light over the entire scene, with the colours of the sky shifting and changing, as if they were dancing out of happiness for Babis and Lakis.

The carefully crafted set up with aerial silks and fabrics added a touch of magic before the altar with the rainbow-coloured flowers. The silks were moving gently in the breeze, creating a soft, ethereal movement, capturing the imagination and inspiring a sense of wonder. All around the ceremony area, different lanterns and candles were placed on the sand creating a romantic ambiance.

The guests were mainly close friends of Babis and Lakis. They had both decided to exclude relatives from their special day. They knew very well that they would only be there to criticise them and spread their negativity like a virus to all the other guests too.

All thirty guests had arrived at the beach, to celebrate their good friends joy. All bare foot with light summer clothing on. The couple had advised them that they didn't expect any formalities and protocols to be followed by anyone, it was just a celebration of love and life.

The atmosphere was charged with excitement and anticipation as all the guests socialised with each another, chatting and laughing, while they were waiting for the couple to arrive. The sound of the waves crashing against the shore in combination with the DJ playing lounge music in the background, crafted an ambiance of tranquillity and serenity for this event.

The warm Greek sun with the sea sparkling in the distance, were adding to the idyllic atmosphere. While the guests sipped on their cocktails from the Athenian mixologist and nibbled on the Greek themed canapés, they were exchanging stories and jokes from their friendship with Lakis and Babis, showing a real sense of closeness and camaraderie amongst them. Most of them were close friends and members of the Greek LGBTQ community. They were sharing so many common experiences between them, living in the conservative and, most of the times, narrow-minded Greek society.

Soula, Barbara, Eleni and Vasilis had created their own little group while waiting for their boys to turn up.

"Isn't it fantastic? What a scene!" said Barbara.

"Oh, truly incredible! This place is straight out of a fantasy book!" replied Eleni with a big smile on her face, holding

Vasilis' hand.

"And very well done to both of you! What you have put together today is just outstanding! How hard it must have been to just move everything to this remote beach? It's just unbelievable!!" complimented Barbara in full excitement.

"It was really, really, really hard work, I can admit that. And don't get me started about what we had to go through to finally get the permission from the local authority... We've been tortured for months. They asked us for anything they could think of. Each time something new. It was just their way of raising the price for the final bribe they received. If it was for anyone else, we would have aborted the efforts many months ago. But Babis and Lakis are both special to us. And the love between them is so inspiring! Eleni and I would never let the boys down on their special day!" said Vasilis feeling emotional but also accomplished at the same time.

He then turned to Soula who was watching then quietly all this time, still drinking the same first glass of wine since she arrived. "Why are you so quiet? Come on! It's a celebration today! 'Yia Mas' to our boys!" he said and raised his Margarita cocktail on the air.

"Yia Mas!" exclaimed both Barbara and Eleni in synchronisation and raised their cocktail glasses close to Vasilis glass. Soula looked at all of them. Her eyes gave out a feeling of internal apprehension. She finally raised her wine glass and followed the rest three. "Yia Mas." she said in an almost whispering voice.

"What's up Soula? Are you still worried about the date today?" asked Vasils.

"How can I not be worried?? I've never heard of a wedding on Tuesday the 13th. Never. It's such an unlucky day. Oh God! Please protect our boys today!" she said looking straight up to the sky and making the sign of cross to herself with her right hand.

"Kala krasia! (Καλά κρασιά!) [literal translation: good wines. When you hear the Greeks saying this, don't be confused. They're

not wishing the success of any wine product before the harvest of the grapes. They use this expression ironically for someone who talks without relation to the subject of the discussion and seems to be out of place and time.] Come on Soula! Are you still thinking about this stupid superstition? I've told you again and again; forget about it and don't be a killjoy. Anyway, this isn't a typical Greek Orthodox wedding and luckily enough, none of these wild-goat-looking priests are invited. So, this is a superstition-free area. Ok? The boys will exchange their vows and we'll all celebrate with them. That's all. We are here to create no trouble. Your God will protect us today Soula. Don't you believe this after all the prayers you have made to Him?" asked Vasilis semi-sarcastically, semi-exhausted and semi-compassionately.

"I'm still praying for both our boys. Even now that we're talking. Oh God! Protect them today, this Tuesday the 13th..." replied Soula with her head raised to the sky for one more time.

All three of them laughed and moved closer to her. They gave her a team hug to calm her down and help her forget about this silly Greek superstition that had been haunting her like a demon since the day the boys announced the date to her.

As the moment for Lakis and Babis to appear and exchange their vows was approaching, the guests grew quiet and reverent, focusing on the meaningfulness of this sweet anticipation. They all eagerly awaited the arrival of their two beloved people who were about to make a lifelong commitment to each other.

The tension had built up and there was a sense of electricity in the air while everyone waited with bated breath for the ceremony to begin. The music had stopped and the only sound that could be heard was the gentle crash of the waves on the shore.

At last, the moment everyone had been waiting for arrived.

Babis and Lakis appeared!

The DJ put the couple's favourite tune and turned up

the volume. Everyone erupted into cheers and applause, welcoming them with open arms and hearts. They both looked so happy, so fulfilled, so in love! Their hands were intertwined, their eyes locked on each other. They walked barefoot on the soft sand, feeling the warmth of the sun, the breeze of the sea and the unlimited love of their people. They made their way to the altar, where their best friend Tasos was waiting, ready to officiate their union.

Along the way, they greeted their guests with joyful waves and smiles that lit up their faces like fireworks on a starry night. They looked like two little boys who had just being given the best ice cream in the world, in the hottest day of the summer.

Now the celebration of love and commitment could truly begin.

When they reached the altar where the final stage of their connection was about to take place, they both hugged Tasos simultaneously. They stayed like this for a full minute, making all their guests cheer even louder. It was such a euphoric and emotional moment for the three lifelong friends!

Tears in their eyes appeared and they didn't seem they wanted to let go of this magical moment. When they finally finished this historic hug, Lakis and Babis positioned themselves opposite each other to allow the ceremony to start.

Suddenly, out of nowhere, the mood was shattered by the sound of heavy shouting.

"Faggooots!"

"Faggooots!"

"Fuckin gaaaays!"

"Die cocksuckers!"

"You sinners!"

"God will send you to hell to burn!"

"Get out of our island sinners! "

"Get the hell out of here filthy gays!"

"Porthoussa island is not made for faggots like you!"

"Burn to hell all of you filthy gays!"

Twelve hot-headed local men and a Christian Orthodox priest, who seemed to be their leader, had appeared behind the rocks and shouted extreme abuse towards the couple and their guests.

Everyone was shocked and frightened. They didn't expect anything like this by any means.

Babis turned to Lakis. "Don't be afraid babe. These dickheads cannot destroy our special day."

The priest dressed in full-black was standing at the front and centre of the angry mob of the manic Christian Orthodox fanatics. He was the maestro in a symphony of wild beasts ready to devour their prey. The shouting grew louder and louder. With a violent movement of his right hand, holding a wooden cross with Jesus on it and pointing towards the sky, the twelve savages started throwing stones, mainly towards the altar where Tasos was standing with Babis and Lakis.

Everyone dropped down, trying to cover themselves from the menacing stones that plummeted from the heavens. The stones of various sizes landed violently on the sand with savage force, but mainly in a safe distance from the altar.

These hot-headed men seemed more interested in intimidating the crowd than causing physical harm to them. However, survival instincts screamed through everyone's veins and their hearts were pounding like war drums in their chests. It felt as if they were in an actual war zone in Bagdad, Iraq.

And suddenly, there was deadly silence. The thirteen men had disappeared like smoke, in the same way they appeared.

"NOOOOOOOOOO!!!" a deafening scream came out of Lakis mouth.

Everyone froze.

It was Babis.

One of the stones had hit him on the back of his head. The impact was bone-crushing. Blood was gushing out of his head. His massive body crumpled instantaneously and the crimson liquid erupting from his head, painted a macabre scene of bloody carnage on the sand around his skull.

Everyone rushed around him in terror.

Lakis was on his knees next to Babis' collapsing body, holding him in his arms. He collapsed in a sobbing heap next to his fatally wounded other-half.

"Please!! Don't leave me my love!! Dooon't!! Noooo!!" screamed Lakis in despair with whatever oxygen was left in his lungs from crying relentlessly.

Babis was unable to speak any words and struggled to breath. His eyes were slightly open, without blinking. His pupils were enlarged and fixed on Lakis' eyes.

"My Babis... Please stay with me... I love you... Don't go... Please my love..." said Lakis very slowly, struggling to complete his sentence as he cried heavily.

Babis' mouth was slightly open, looking like he was trying to say something. But he didn't. He just took his last breath on the beach in Lakis' hands.

"Forever... and... always..." Lakis, crying his heart out, spoke for the last time to his childhood love.

This time the stone found its target. The injury on Babis' head was so severe that there was no chance to survive from it.

The same happened to their love.

It was bloody Tuesday the 13th.

About The Author

Dino Kottis

Dino Kottis was born in 1979 in Greece. He lived there until the age of 32, when he moved to the UK. He lives in Liverpool with his wife, two daughters and their dog. He has already published two non-fiction books, "Hospitality KnowHow" and "Customer Service Express". "A Greek Bloody Drama" is his first novel.

Printed in Great Britain
by Amazon